14,99

REINCARNATION
ANGELS, DEMONS AND GHOSTS

REINCARNATION
ANGELS, DEMONS AND GHOSTS

According to the *Zohar* and *Kabbalah*

By
Jill Amar

Including excerpts of Rabbi Elyahu Kin's Lectures

Order this book online at www.trafford.com
or email orders@trafford.com

Most Trafford titles are also available at major online book retailers.

Printed in the United States of America.

ISBN: 978-1-4669-7981-9 (sc)
ISBN: 978-1-4669-7983-3 (hc)
ISBN: 978-1-4669-7982-6 (e)

Library of Congress Control Number: 2013902145

Trafford rev. 02/05/2013

 www.trafford.com

North America & international
toll-free: 1 888 232 4444 (USA & Canada)
phone: 250 383 6864 ♦ fax: 812 355 4082

I want to thank God the Almighty for assisting me in writing this book. I also would like to thank Rabbi Elyahu Kin from the bottom of my heart, who encouraged me greatly to do so, and gave me permission to use material from his lectures to make this work come to fruition.

I hope this book will contribute to your spiritual and personal growth, and will achieve its purpose.

With all my love and best wishes for each and everyone of you.

Jill Amar, Los Angeles, CA, 2009

Contents

CHAPTER ONE

What is a soul?

"Vayomer Elohim Naasse Adam Betzalmeinu Kidmuteinu . . ." (Genesis 1:26) And God said "Let us make man in our form and image" . . .

"Let us" . . . . God said that to the angels. *Rashi* explains that the plural (let us) is used to indicate that God sought the counsel of the angels before creating man. Given the infinite wisdom of God, seeking counsel was totally unnecessary, and God did so only to teach us humility. To teach us that regardless of how wise one may be, one should always be ready to listen to the advice of one's inferiors. A person who is vain, and apt to have an insatiable ego is likely to consider accepting advice from anyone of lesser status as degrading and demeaning.

The commentaries point out that a vain person not only fails to benefit from the opinions of others, but by his implicit rejection of *Rashi's* interpretation of "Let us make man", he is left with no alternative but to explain the words "Let us" as referring to a plurality of Gods, because if the Creator was not seeking the advice of His inferiors, He must have been requesting the participation of an equal.

The *Midrash* states that when God sought the counsel of the angels on creating man, two opposing opinions were offered: the angel of *Chesed* (kindness) and the angel of *Tzedek* (justice) were in favor of man's creation, because man is by nature kind and just. The angel of *Emet* (truth) and the angel of *Shalom* (peace) opposed man's creation,

1

arguing that man is deceitful and argumentative. God then cast the angel of truth down to earth and created man without opposition. How could it be if the angel of peace remained to object? Because once truth is cast aside, it is simple to achieve peace.

"Vyetzar Hashem Elohim et HaAdam Aafar Min Haadama Vyefach Be'apav Nishmat Chaim Vayihi HaAdam Lenefesh Chaya" . . . (Genesis 2:7)—God fashioned man dust from the earth, and blew into his nostrils a living soul, and man became a living being . . . .

Like all other creatures, man was fashioned from the elements. His distinguishing feature is that God instilled a soul within him.

Man's ability to make free moral choices is of greater importance than his intellect. Animals are dominated by their biological drives which they are helpless to resist. The only reason an animal will forgo gratification of a biological drive is if it fears punishment, and not because of any moral choice.

Hence, if the only reason a person refrains from gratifying a physical drive is because of fear of punishment or social sanction, he has not yet advanced beyond animal behavior.

It is unlikely that any animal has ever paused to reflect on the purpose of its existence. The search for the meaning of life is thus exclusively a human feature, and is therefore a defining characteristic of humanity. These are the characteristics that comprise the spirit with which man was endowed, and it is the spirit which defines man and sets him apart from other creatures.

And God said "Let us make man in our form and image" . . . God has no form nor does He have an image. Therefore, we shouldn't take these words literally. They obviously mean something else.

In our form means that Man will resemble the angels in that he will have a soul. He will walk on two feet, unlike animals which walk on four feet, and he will face up.

In our image means that Man will be endowed with the ability to comprehend and have intelligence. What is the purpose and the need for man to have these abilities? So he can have the capability to choose and have the free will to choose between good or evil.

Animals for instance live and are governed by their instincts. Humans on the other hand, whom decisions' process stems from their intelligence, are responsible and accountable for their actions. They choose to do good or evil out of their own free will. These "tools" are given to us through the soul. The soul is so to speak the captain of the ship.

God created Adam from the dust of the earth. The word Adam is derived from two Hebrew words: *Adamah*—earth, and *Dam*—blood. Adam was created from the earth or the dust of the earth, and from blood. The *Zohar* tells us that blood is what sustains life. Earth and blood are the physical elements of a human being.

God Himself created man unlike all other creatures, which were brought forth by the earth. Since God created the earth, He also is the Creator of all other creatures. God was much more involved personally in creating human beings. Humans are above all other creations. God Himself blew in man's nostrils a living soul. Just like a glassblower would blow his own breath into the glass, so did God blow his own breath into Adam. Adam has within himself a part of God—His breath. The *Zohar* says that the human soul is a divine part from above.

The word *Neshamah*—soul, comes from the word *Neshimah*—breath. In Judaism, the death of a person is determined by whether the person still breathes or not. If there is no breath, there is no need to check for a pulse or brainwaves.

What is the soul comprised of? The *Kabbalah* tells us that the soul consists of five parts: *Nefesh, Ruach, Neshamah, Chayah* and *Yechidah*. The first three parts, the *Nefesh, Ruach* and *Nesamah* are the parts many people are familiar with. *Chayah* and *Yechidah* are the parts the majority of people never heard of.

There is a verse in *Mishlei*, written by King Salomon that states: "*Ner Hashem Nishmat Adam*"—God's candle is the human soul. King Salomon goes on to elaborate about the quality of the soul. He compares it to a candle. Just like a candle illuminates a room, the soul illuminates the entire body.

The Kabbalah also mentions different kind of lights: *Or Pnimi*— Internal light, *Or Yashar*—Direct light, *Or Makif*—Surrounding light, and *Or Ein Sof*—Infinite light. The *Kabbalah* is not referring here to physical light, but spiritual light.

These lights illuminate and envelop the human body. The *Nefesh*, *Ruach* and *Neshamah* are influenced by internal spiritual lights.

The *Chayah* and *Yechidah* are influenced by external spiritual lights, outside our bodies.

Let us start by exploring the *Nefesh* part of our souls.

The *Nefesh* is our soul's lowest form. The *Nefesh* is often associated with the word *Behemi*—animal. The *Nefesh* is our animal spirit. This animal spirit contains all the earthly desires such as eating, drinking, sleeping etc. to enjoy life. The Torah says that blood is *Nefesh*. Our blood is the "engine" that gives us the drive to do things.

All three, the *Nefesh*, *Ruach* and *Neshamah* are within our bodies, but each one has a separate physical dwelling. The *Nefesh* dwells in our liver. The *Nefesh* is affected by our actions and is the closest to our physical essence. The soul's portion mostly affected by our good or bad deeds is the *Nefesh*. The *Nefesh* is associated with *Olam Ha'Assyah*—the world of action. The *Kabbalah* tells us that the essence of the *Nefesh* is a desire to receive. The *Neshamah* part essence's, on the other hand, is to give and do for others. The *Ruach* part of the soul—the spirit—is in between the *Nefesh* and the *Neshamah*, and acts as a mediator which ties them together.

The *Nefesh* is tied to the body, the *Neshamah* is more spiritual, and the *Ruach* bridges between them.

Let us now explore the *Ruach* part of our soul.

The *Ruach* is the driving force behind our emotions, which as we know are not physical.

When we are happy or sad, arrogant or jealous, fearful or in love, it is our *Ruach* expressing itself. The *Ruach* is one step higher than the physical *Nefesh*. Where does the *Ruach* dwell in our bodies? In the heart. Like the *Nefesh* rules the world of action, the *Ruach* rules the world of speech, which is the next elevated level after our deeds. The ability of speech was given to man by God to communicate, unlike animals who lack that ability.

The third part of our soul which stands at a higher spiritual level is the *Neshamah*. The *Neshamah* is the part that controls the mind. The intellectual part. It's above the deeds, feelings and emotions. The *Neshamah's* dwelling in our body is our brain.

The brain controls our thoughts. Everything starts with our thoughts. Our thoughts dictate our actions and deeds, our emotions and feelings. Our thoughts create our speech—what we say, and our actions—what we do.

Let's move on to the *Chayah* and *Yechidah*.

Both *Chayah* and *Yechidah* illuminate from the outside and have a totally different function.

Chayah—life, sustenance. The soul receives the nourishment from above at all times. It is as if there is an unbilical cord connected from our soul to the upper worlds, and we are constantly fed spiritually so to speak.

Yechidah—unit. The *Yechidah* is God's energy. According to our sages, the *Chayah* and *Yechidah* illuminate when the individual performs good deeds and effect him in a certain way.

In most texts, we will read about the *Neshamah* part of the soul. They rarely mention the terms *Chayah* and *Yechidah*.

The *Neshamah* represents the spiritual aspect of humans as opposed to the physical aspect.

CHAPTER TWO

Neshamot—Souls

There are various kinds, levels, and categories of souls.

Where do souls come from? According to the *Kabbalah*, they come from a tree of souls which has branches. Because souls come from different branches in the tree of souls, their mission is different and specific to them. That is why one will choose to become a Rabbi or a Priest, a teacher, a scientist or an architect. According to the root of his soul, the individual chooses what he needs to do in life in order to fulfill his mission.

When two people for instance are from the same soul root, they instantly feel a connection and a certain closeness. Sometimes, we encounter people for the first time in our life, and with no rational explanation, feel that instant connection for no apparent reason.

How does the soul enter the body?

If it is the soul's first and initial incarnation, the body is capable to receive all three parts, *Nefesh*, *Ruach* and *Neshamah*.

All of us have the lowest level of *Nefesh* within us. However, if one performs good deeds, he merits the illumination of his *Ruach* and *Neshamah* portions of his soul. The majority of us have the basic *Nefesh* unless it is our first incarnation, which is very rare.

How could this be? If the majority of us possess only the *Nefesh*, how do we have the ability to have feelings and emotions, comprehend and have intelligence which enable us to make our choices, which are controlled by the *Ruach* and *Neshamah*?

According to the *Kabbalah,* the answer to that is that the *Ruach* and *Neshamah* are included as well in the *Nefesh.*

The *Nefesh*, the driving force of the human body, the same *Nefesh* has the *Nefesh* of the *Nefesh*, the *Ruach* of the *Nefesh*, and the *Neshamah* of the *Nefesh*. The same *Nefesh* that we all possess is subdivided into these three expressions.

We can acquire the *Ruach* and *Neshamah* portions of our soul according to, and depending on our good deeds and actions. Sometimes, when a soul is reincarnated, all three parts will come down and dwell in their bodies.

The *Nefesh* is the portion of the soul that hovers over the grave for twelve months after we die, and is very dear and precious to God. After the twelve months period is over, every year at the date of the deceased death, if you visit his grave, his *Nefesh* can hear you. Even though our body goes into a grave when we die, our *Ruach* goes back to God. The body decomposes in the grave and the spirit remains. The decomposed body will resurrect eventually when the resurrection of the dead will occur at the end of days.

The *Zohar* states that there is such a thing called "vapors of the bones" in the grave, which applies only to the graves of the righteous people. In Judaism, many Jews go visit the Holy righteous Rabbis' graves to pray for their needs. The vapor of their bones so to speak is still there, and in the merit of these righteous souls, God listens to their prayers.

The *Ruach* portion of the soul, if the person was at a *Ruach* level, goes to the lower paradise, and the *Neshamah* portion of the soul goes to the higher paradise.

When does the *Nefesh* enter the body? According to the *Kabbalah*, the *Neshamah* part enters the body at the time of conception. That is when the person's destiny is determined and the kind of life he or she will have. The *Nefesh* portion of the soul grows with the fetus. Another Kabbalistic opinion says that the *Nefesh* comes into play at the very end, when the baby is born.

According to the *Zohar*, as soon as the baby's head comes out, a *Tselem* (shadow), which protects the individual, comes along with it and envelops the body for thirty days after birth and then leaves it.

Dreams

Which part of the soul dreams when we dream?

Is it the *Nefesh*, *Ruach* or *Neshamah* part of our soul that dreams? It depends on a few factors. Every night, our soul goes up to heaven and reports all of its deeds for the day. The soul is the decision maker of all its deeds. The *Neshamah* part is the part capable of soaring the highest in heaven. The *Nefesh* and *Ruach* parts cannot reach those highs.

When our dreams are fantasy, or the manifestation of our thoughts or what we had to eat all day, then it is the *Nefesh* portion who is dreaming. The *Nefesh* portion of our soul corresponds to and is affected by our thoughts and the food we eat. Therefore, accordingly, these dreams are meaningless.

Dreams that contains a real message, a premonition, come from the higher heaven and stem from the *Neshamah* portion of the soul.

CHAPTER THREE

Reincarnation

Transcript of Rabbi Elyahu Kin's lectures

Reincarnation is a phenomenon which offers one of the best documented and most compelling proofs for the eternal nature of the human soul. Large numbers of scientifically researched accounts offer credible evidence that human beings can actually remember experiences from previous lives—circumstances in which they lived as a different person in a vastly different time and place. Details of these descriptions have been researched and found to be true, though they contain information that would have been impossible for the individuals relating them to have known.

Belief in reincarnation exists in many traditions, including Hinduism, Buddhism, the Druze tradition, and others. In many cases, reincarnation is understood to be part of a never ending cycle of death and rebirth. The *Kabbalah* states that a person is reincarnated only for a special reason.

According to the *Kabbalah*, God's goal in creating the world was in order to bestow goodness upon His creation. And since the perfect and infinite Creator seeks to bestow a goodness that is perfect, he created human beings as essentially spiritual creatures.

In the words of the *Arizal*, from the beginning of his book *Sha'ar Ha-Gilgulim* (Gate of reincarnation):

"Know that the essential human being is a spiritual entity, within a material body. The body is a garment of the person, but not the person himself". This is because every bodily or material pleasure is limited.

Spiritual pleasure and delight reach beyond all limitations or restrictions. Thus, God created man as a spiritual entity—so that he should be a vessel capable of receiving and experiencing spiritual pleasure.

When a person is born, his or her spiritual essence is a kind of raw material which must be shaped and formed into an active spiritual vessel.

This raw material contains 248 parts and 365 connectors and switches. For this reason, the Sages have stated that the human body has 248 limbs and 365 sinews (ligaments). So too, the Torah—the "operating manual" granted to humankind on Mount Sinai—contains 613 commandments: 248 positive commandments and 365 prohibitions.

By virtue of following the "manufacturer's instructions", the material and spiritual limbs are enlightened and the human being becomes a spiritual vessel capable of connecting to its Creator and receiving the ultimate good, which is the purpose of creation. (Note that non-Jews are as beloved and precious to God as all creatures formed in His image, as the *mishnah* states:

"Beloved is a human being created in His image").

As mentioned before, each component of the soul (*nefesh, ruach, neshama*) has a purpose. Every soul is unique and has a specific mission.

Since the soul cannot be seen due to its spiritual nature, we must find scientific proof that there is something else besides the physical body.

Jews believe that the soul survives after we die, and moves on to another dimension, a dimension called *Olam Haneshamot*—the world of souls, spirits.

It is a fascinating world containing ghosts, *gehenom* (temporary hell), and *Gan Eden* (the garden of Eden—paradise). According to the *kabbalah*, we have a way of knowing what goes on in that dimension with testimonies that can be proven in multiple ways, including scientifically.

All souls are special because they are divine, and a part of God. Every human being on this planet was created in the image of God.

Every individual soul has a mission. All souls, collectively, have a common mission: *Lishmor Al Hagan*—to maintain the Garden of Eden.

When God created Adam, He placed him in the garden of Eden and commanded him to watch over the garden. Adam represents all of humanity—the entire human race—Our task is to preserve this wonderful, beautiful world that God created.

We have the ability to either maintain it, or to ruin and destroy it, with the free will which God gave us.

Free will is very powerful and can be dangerous and destructive at times, when misused. Whether it's in a form of a nuclear bomb, or the decrease of the ozone layers due to smog etc . . . it is up to us what we do with our free will.

God has no interest in destroying this beautiful world. Unfortunately, humanity *can* be destructive.

The common goal of all souls in this world is to take care of our planet. To maintain the balance that God created, in making sure that the evil forces of impurity do not overcome the forces of purity and goodness. Not allowing the forces of evil to take over and tip the balance.

This mission is common to all of humanity.

According to Judaism, God gave Jews a mission when they received the Torah on Mount Sinai. God told them that there is a thing called *Chet HaAdam Harishon*—the first and original sin of Adam—

The first sin is not merely a story documented in Genesis about a serpent seducing or misleading Eve, which in turn mislead Adam to eat the fruit from the forbidden tree.

There is an important symbolism and a tremendous message here for all humanity. The message that man has the ability to rebel against God's instructions, God's plan, God's blueprint.

Unfortunately, that is exactly what happened with Adam and Eve.

As a result of their disobedience, the world is in an imperfect state. A state where we have the ability to go against God's will, thus, against his plan and design.

God commanded the Jewish people *Letaken Olam Bemalchut Shaddai*—to repair and fix the world and bring it to the level that He wanted it to be initially, which is a perfect state of harmony reigning in this world.

Since unfortunately, we didn't fulfill this task too well, it will be done by God Himself and the Messiah. That is not to say that no good at all was done in this world.

However, there are many problems in this world, across the globe, whether it is wars, famine or dishonesty, with all religions and all faiths.

Human beings still have the same problems they had more or less in the past. We are selfish and can be destructive. Every soul has its specific mission and can contribute to the world if it chooses to.

Some people choose not to contribute and not to fulfill their mission, therefore, there must be a mechanism in place to allow repair.

For example, the human body has a built in mechanism called the immune system. When the immune system senses a foreign body that wants to invade a healthy person's body, it will counter attack that foreign body with its built in mechanism.

The body is able to fight off any "enemies" that come to invade and undo the balance. Sometimes it will succeed and sometimes it won't. It all depends on what overpowers what.

God had to create a mechanism in the same manner with creation. A mechanism that would fix things. This mechanism consists of two parts:

Midat Hadin—measure of judgment—and *Midat Harachamim*— measure of mercy—

The measure of judgment may sound a bit harsh, as in punishment. However, it is not harsh punishment the way we understand it. God is good and compassionate, and all He wants for us is good.

The whole act of creating the world was an act of goodness and kindness. So when we say "judgment", we mean a mechanism to enable repair. God wants to repair what has been corrupted and undone. He does it by way of judgment which balances everything out. There are multiple kinds of judgments.

On the other hand, the measure of mercy, or the measure of compassion, means that God allows the human being himself to fix what needs to be fixed. God is kind of saying: "I am not going to fix it. I am not going to use the measure of judgment. I want **you** to fix it".

God is very patient and gives a person a chance for many years to fix it himself, using the measure of mercy, because He knows that each person has the potential to fix it himself.

The essence of the measure of mercy is actually, repentance.

God is very tolerant and kind, and allows the person to repent.

Sometimes, we may see wicked people who get away with almost anything.

Some of them may be prosperous, have a comfortable life and everything seems to run smoothly in their life. But, don't let appearances fool you.

In order to really comprehend the Reward and Punishment "system", one must know a person's life in details from the moment he or she was born until the day he or she died, including his or her previous incarnations.

"Repairing" the world is crucial because if man was given permission to do anything he wanted, he could destroy the world, if he chose to. God doesn't allow these types of people to have power because they can destroy the world.

King Salomon said that the heart of kings is in God's hands. One may have a tremendous amount of free will in certain areas in life. Kings and rulers have less of it because they bear great responsibilities for their entire country. They just cannot do whatever they want.

They have free will, but God doesn't allow them to do whatever they please because they can potentially destroy their country and go against HIS will.

Therefore, if for instance things go awfully wrong, God created a mechanism that stops it from becoming worse. That's when the measure of judgment comes into play.

The damage inflicted can be upon the human being himself or upon the world. Just as people can harm their bodies for instance, by smoking or overeating, they can harm their souls as well. The damage done is to the balance in this world.

When the balance scale tips to the evil side, the result will be for instance many wars in the world, famine in some parts of the world, terrorism, of which we are all too familiar with unfortunately.

The Torah is a guideline, a road map so to speak for the Jewish nation. It tells us how to live our lives successfully, how to arrive to our destination, how to fulfill our mission—our own individual mission as well as the mission of our nation.

The most effective and powerful form of method to correct one's way and fulfill one's individual mission and correction of the soul, is by way of reincarnation.

It is the mechanism that God put in place to restore something that got out of balance, that has gone wrong, for the individual as well as for the collective whole.

As we mentioned before, the body is a garment for the eternal soul that inhabits it. So what we have to rectify is our soul and not our body, since our soul is the decision maker and the "captain of the ship" who directs the body.

Both body and soul are responsible for our actions. However, it is the soul's task to do the "repair", the correction of what has gone wrong and out of balance.

The reincarnation of the soul in a different body and a different lifetime, for as many times as is needed to undo what went wrong, is a mechanism that God put in place as an opportunity for us to repair.

The component of the soul that comes back in reincarnation to do the correction, is the part called the *nefesh*. The *nefesh* is in charge of the body, therefore it is the part of the soul to "blame" so to speak.

The *ruach* and *neshama* parts of the souls are generally not involved. Sometimes however, they will come back with the *nefesh* in a reincarnation.

Judaism was introduced to, and made aware of the concept of reincarnation, only when the *Zohar* came out. Until then, reincarnation was an esoteric secret topic that was known and shared among the few who knew and practiced *kabbalah*.

When the *Zohar* made us aware of it, it shed some light into many difficult incomprehensible situations. Some situations that would appear as unfair to us became understood and more acceptable.

For instance, the untimely and premature death of a young person, who might reincarnate in a different country, with different circumstances, may be more bearable and easier to accept.

The teachings on reincarnation answer many of life's most enduring questions, and touch upon ancient mysteries: Why do bad things happen to good people? Why do good things happen to bad people?

The truth is that only God knows who is truly righteous and who is truly evil. And only He knows what is really good and bad for each person. Even a truly righteous person may have to repay, in this world, a debt acquired in a previous lifetime. This world refines him as well, so that he can achieve the spiritual perfection for which he was created.

When we are aware of the concept of reincarnation, we may be able to understand a person's destiny, customized and determined at the time of conception, based on the person's previous life/lives. Otherwise, why would someone be born destined to be poor and others destined to be wealthy?

We know of people who are billionaires who never even went to college. Some of them barely speak English. That is due to destiny. A great deal of a person's destiny is determined by his previous incarnations.

A person's destiny was customized to bring about the soul's correction of what needed to be rectified from a previous incarnation. For example, if a person in a previous lifetime was very wealthy, and money "went up to his head", and consequently, he committed many sins, this time around, he could be born with the destiny of not having money, or could be born destined to have money again, but will be presented with the same challenges to get the chance to correct and not to repeat the same mistakes he has made in his previous incarnation.

Only God knows best how to bring about the best opportunities to repair one's deeds from previous lifetimes.

Another form of "repair" or correction, besides reincarnation, is *gehenom*—temporary hell.

It is not purgatory as many of us would think. It is a kind of burning hot shower (not literally), a kind of laundrymat for a lack of a better term, where the souls get cleansed.

In reality, the soul itself begs to be cleansed. The *Zohar* explains that the soul cannot bear to face the *Shechinah*—Divine Presence—with all its "stains". The soul feels very "dirty" and is pained when having to face the *Shechinah*.

Imagine a bride on her wedding day, walking into the wedding hall with ketchup stains all over her dress. Imagine her embarrassment.

The embarrassment that the soul experiences when it is soiled with bad deeds that it cannot deny, since there is no way it can lie in the supernal courts, **is** the actual hell.

Sometimes, we will experience minor atonements while "repairing", such as painful experiences of illnesses, or financial hardships which are called *kappara*—an atonement for our sins, which in turn enabled us to make the rectification needed for our souls.

It is actually the measure of judgment that God brought upon us because we didn't rectify what needed to be rectified on our own.

Reincarnation is by far the best form of "repair", because it gives the person a brand new chance to start from scratch.

Having the chance to come back and being reincarnated several times, gives a person the chance to compile and accumulate "credits". There is no way one can incur more "debits" when reincarnated, because the portion of the soul that comes back is the exact and specific portion of the soul that needed to still correct some specific deeds.

The portion of the soul that was good and did everything well, does not come down, and stays in the upper realms.

It may be difficult to comprehend because we do not understand how a soul, as a whole, can split itself. It is because the soul is comprised of components of which some stay in the upper realms and some get reincarnated.

King Salomon compared the soul to a lit candle. Why? Because with one original lit candle, you can light many more candles which won't diminish the light of that original candle.

The original candle wasn't wasted in any way by lighting others with it. The original flame will always be there, regardless of how many candles you light with it. Therefore, the soul can split itself.

All of these soul parts are called according to *kabbalah* *"nitzotzot"*— sparks.

The portion of the soul being reincarnated is one spark of that soul.

Usually, a reincarnation can occur 4 times. The original, initial incarnation, plus 3 more times. If after 4 times the soul didn't achieve the correction that was needed, it doesn't get another chance to reincarnate.

How can that be? Most of us have been reincarnated more than 4 times. The reason for that is that once we start and keep on repairing with each incarnation, we can come back to continue the correction process in progress.

A reincarnation can manifest from the highest level of a human being, to lower levels of animal, plant, or inanimate objects.

When reincarnated into the lower levels of animal, plant or inanimate objects, the reincarnation is usually for a short period of time—days, weeks, months, or a few years—and as we know, the manifestation of a reincarnation as a human can last many years, a full life, a few years, or even a few days.

When the soul accomplishes its correction mission, it then passes away.

Another form of reincarnation is called *"Ibur"*—or impregnated reincarnation.

For example: Let's say Simon is a person alive, and another soul goes into his body, because Simon is about to perform a good deed and the additional soul which entered him needed that exact same good deed to be rectified. It could inhabit Simon's body for weeks or months.

Sometimes, that additional soul would enter Simon's body to guide him with a certain thing, which in itself is another kind of *Ibur*.

What is the difference between an *Ibur* reincarnation and a conventional one?

With the conventional reincarnation, one is not aware of the fact that he has been reincarnated. With the *Ibur* reincarnation, the person knows that he is "piggy backing" so to speak another soul.

A man can come back in a reincarnation as a woman and vice-versa. It doesn't happen often. When a man is being reincarnated as a woman, the woman cannot get pregnant.

A reincarnation can occur right after the person's death, or it can occur after many years.

Why would a soul come back after many years?

Because in the upper realms, the soul keeps on getting elevated to higher levels. When the soul wishes to keep rising to a higher level where it is not allowed to enter until it corrects certain things, it is asked to reincarnate to correct first what needs to be corrected, so it could enter the higher dimension level it wished to.

It is very important in Jewish law to bury the dead right away, because the soul cannot come back if it needs to be reincarnated until the "old" body is buried. It is called *Kevod Hamet*—respect of the dead.

Some souls however, cannot come back right away.

These souls are in a dimension called *kaf hakela*—the "sling shot"—of which we'll speak about in a later chapter. If a reincarnation is necessary for these souls, when they are finished with the "sling shot" phase, they will reincarnate.

We would think that reincarnation can apply to both men and women as well, since it is the process of the correction of the soul.

Our sages tell us that men who study Torah do a lot of their soul correction work by the mere fact that the Torah protects them from *Gehenom*. Since men cannot cleanse their souls in *Gehenom*, the only way for them to be able to rectify their souls is by being reincarnated.

Sometimes, when a righteous man needs to be reincarnated to correct minor things, God will allow his soul mate to be reincarnated so he could be with her. Sometimes, only a spark of his soul mate will reincarnate.

The question that often arises is: If souls are being reincarnated in different bodies, what will happen when God will resurrect the dead? Which body will arise? How can all the bodies arise when it is one soul only?

The *Zohar* addresses this question and says that since the soul can split into several sparks, all the reincarnated bodies that are deserving to rise will rise. They will get a brand new body, a new *nefesh* and will share the same soul.

The sages tell us that a person who never had children will surely be reincarnated. That person has to come back so he could have continuity by having children.

Most reincarnated people do not know or remember who they were in their previous incarnation, nor do they know what needs to be accomplished to achieve their soul's correction. However, many great Jewish figures have claimed to remember their previous incarnations, including particular details of past lives, and even the spiritual rectification (*tikkun*) for which they returned to this world.

There have been those of great spiritual power who could even recognize the previous lives of others and what they needed to fix. The *Arizal* was one of them.

So, how can one accomplish what needs to be done if one doesn't know?

Our soul is our guide. Our soul will guide us to meet the exact people we have to meet. It will present the exact circumstances needed to make our soul's correction because God wants us to rectify.

The following true stories will attest to the fact that reincarnation exists.

This story occurred in a small town in New York called New Square.

A Jewish fish store owner had many employees, and one of them was from Puerto Rico. This Puerto Rican employee went to the back of the store one day to prepare some *gefilte fish*, as he would normally do.

As he was busily working, he suddenly heard a fish talking in a human voice. He got so scared and in panic, ran out and told his boss: "The devil is in the store" to which the boss replied: "What are you talking about?" The employee told him that he heard a fish talk.

The owner of the fish store knew that his employee was sane and reliable, so he went to the back room to check the matter out. The owner heard the voice, and not only that, he even recognized who's voice it was. It was the voice of one of his customers that has passed away, a very good man who was a Torah scholar and had an excellent reputation. He was reincarnated into a fish.

What did the fish say? All he said was: "I am so and so—Get ready. The end of days is coming".

The owner of the store tried to grab the fish but couldn't. The fish jumped into the pool with all the other fishes. The owner decided to make *gefilte fish* out of all the fishes in the pool.

This story was documented in the community newspapers. Many people called the store to verify if indeed it happened, and it was verified by the owner and the Puerto Rican employee.

*   *   *

This next story happened to Rabbi Kin's grandfather.

He was in a Jewish cemetery in Vienna, and there he saw a tombstone shaped like a fish. He wondered why would a tombstone have the shape of a fish.

Since it was a very old cemetery, he went to look at the community archives where they kept documents with unusual and incredible tales that occurred in that specific town.

He checked to see if by any chance there was a story about a tombstone shaped like a fish.

He found out that approximately 300 years ago, a man bought a fish for the Sabbath dinner and brought it home. As he was about to cut it up, the fish started talking and said: "*Shema Israel Adonai Elohenu, Adonai Echad*"—Hear Israel, God is our God, God is One. The man was startled to say the least. He didn't understand what was that all about.

He went to see his rabbi and told him the whole story. His rabbi said to him that it was probably a reincarnated soul and that he should go and bury it. They shaped the tombstone like a fish as a testimony of what happened.

When a soul is reincarnated in a food form, that soul needs to be elevated to a higher level. In order to elevate a soul from food form to a higher form of being, one has to make a blessing on the food. This is one of the reasons that Jews are commanded to make a blessing on food. Our tradition tells us that righteous people are reincarnated into fish, because the fish is purer than an animal. That is why a fish doesn't need to be slaughtered. The element of fish is water, thus it is purer than earth.

Another famous story occurred in the *Arizal* era.

There was a Yeshiva dean who had a daughter and was very concerned about her not being married yet. She was very selective, very intelligent and had a lot going for her, and her father couldn't understand why she was not married yet.

One day, a young man named Abraham arrived in Israel from Spain, right after the Spanish inquisition. He was a *morano (*a Jew who converted to Christianity out of coercion) and he wished to return to his Jewish faith. He was an ignoramus.

He looked for employment and was offered a position at the dean's yeshiva, as a janitor, doing all kinds of odd jobs.

One night, the dean's wife passed away.

She came in a dream to her daughter and told her that her soul mate is the young Spaniard Abraham who works at the yeshiva as a janitor. The daughter was very surprised and perplexed to hear that. Her father, the dean, had the exact same dream.

He obviously had a big problem with it. He was an important rabbi, the dean of a yeshiva, and he was not going to allow his only daughter to marry this young ignoramus.

They shared their dream with one another, and since they both had the same dream, they thought that it could be a true message and a true dream.

Both father and daughter decided to go see the *Arizal*.

As soon as the *Arizal* saw them approaching him, he said to them: "*Mazel Tov!* (congratulations). You don't have to tell me anything. I already know.

Abraham is your son in law and your daughter's soul mate". He then instructed the dean to write down a *ketuba* (marriage license) and to state in it that everything that belongs to him will eventually belong to Abraham after his death, because he is marrying off his only daughter.

The dean couldn't believe what he was hearing. Nevertheless, he greatly respected the *Arizal's* spiritual power and did what the *Arizal* instructed him to do.

His daughter married Abraham, the young ignoramus, and right after the wedding, Abraham asked the dean to move out of his house because everything belongs to him now. He even didn't wait for the dean to pass away. He kicked him out right away.

The dean was very upset and thought to himself: "How can my son in law have the nerve and *chutzpah* to do that to me?" He wondered how could it be? He married off his only daughter to him, a total ignoramus, and then he had the nerve to take all of his money away and kick him out?

He right away went to see the *Arizal* to tell him about it and to get some kind of explanation. With tears in his eyes, he asked him: "what's going on? Why is this happening to me?" The *Arizal* then said to him: "Let me tell you a story.

Once upon a time not too long ago, there was a couple—a husband and wife—the wife was pregnant and would always go see her rabbi and complain about her husband's physical and verbal abuse.

Her rabbi never really believed her because he thought that women often exaggerate certain situations, especially since the husband didn't come across as an abuser. In fact, he was a very nice man.

However, one day, while she was still pregnant, the young woman came to see the rabbi again, and this time, she told him that her husband beat her very hard on her stomach, and as a result, the fetus was aborted due to a miscarriage.

Her rabbi got very upset to hear that and it disturbed him a great deal. In essence, this woman's husband murdered their unborn child.

The rabbi right away went to see her husband and scolded him. He told him he was a terrible person and that he had to divorce his wife.

He went on telling him that his wife doesn't deserve what he put her through and that he has to give her all of his possessions including all of his money.

In reality, the real truth was that the wife herself beat her own stomach very hard, and was willing to lose her unborn baby and blame her husband for it, so she could be with another man.

Eventually, all three of them died—the rabbi, the husband and the wife—

In the Supernal courts, they decreed that everything with this situation was unjust.

They saw that the husband didn't do anything wrong and was blamed for something he didn't do.

They saw that the wife was to blame, and they saw that the rabbi didn't do the right thing. Who gave him the right to take away all of this poor innocent man's possessions and money, and give it to the wife?

The Supernal courts came to the decision that a Major repair is in order. They decided to reincarnate all three of them back to life.

The rabbi who gave away the innocent man's money, this incarnation around will lose the money. The woman who killed her own unborn child will this time around lose her child.

The innocent man who unjustly lost all of his possessions and money will get all of his possessions and money back this time around. This correction process was decreed from above".

By the way, the dean's daughter got pregnant from Abraham her husband a second time and lost her baby.

*　*　*

When a soul gets reincarnated, it is the soul that guides the person to the exact circumstances and people needed in their current lifetime to make their soul correction from previous incarnations.

Moses once asked God to explain His ways to him so he could comprehend them, because he couldn't figure out God.

So God took him behind the scenes of a certain scenario, where Moses could see the whole scenario and the people in the scenario couldn't see him.

God then showed him the scene of a young boy walking in a field. Then, Moses sees a man riding on a horse in the same field who was unaware that his wallet dropped out of his pocket.

The boy walking in the field came upon his wallet and picked it up. Finders keepers.

Later on, Moses sees a poor man walking in the same field, very tired after a long day's labor, who lays down on the grass to take a nap.

A while later, the rider who dropped and lost his wallet, realizes that he doesn't have it. He rides back to where he thinks he might have dropped it and sees the poor man napping on the grass.

He wakes the poor man up and accuses him of taking the wallet that he found on the grass. The poor man rightfully denies it and says that he has no idea of what he is talking about. The rider doesn't believe him, beats the poor man up and consequently kills him.

Moses is watching this whole scene and further tells God that he can't understand what's going on.

He tells God: "I just saw the whole thing. I saw that it was the child who took the rider's wallet and not the poor man. It is not fair that this poor man got killed for something he didn't do".

God then tells Moses: "You didn't see everything. You only saw part of the scene".

To understand it better, imagine someone coming to the movie theatre to see a movie. He walks into the theatre in the middle of the movie, and sees someone getting killed in the movie. He wonders what's going on? Why did this person get killed? The people who saw the movie from its beginning know exactly why this person got killed in the movie.

We come to this earth for 70-80 years or more, or less, and we expect to understand everything that's going on in our lives. However, we only see a "part of the movie".

God then explains to Moses what happened with the horse rider, the young boy and the poor laborer in a previous lifetime.

That young boy's money in a previous incarnation was taken away from him by the horse rider. The poor innocent man that got killed by the rider, in a previous lifetime, got very angry at the wrong man (the horse rider) for some reason and killed him.

That is why he got killed by the rider this time around.

From this we can see that justice is always served eventually.

*   *   *

Here is another true account of reincarnation which was published in India:

"I Remember How I Was Murdered at 5:45"
From the Press Information Bureau, New Delhi, India

On August 28, 1983 at 5:45pm, Suresh Varma, a resident of the city of Agra, India, was murdered. A bullet entered his temple and he was killed instantly. The murderer fled.

Four months later, Tito Singh was born in the very same city of Agra.

When Tito turned six years old he told his parents: "In a previous incarnation, I had a store that sold radios. I remember how I was killed at 5:45pm in the afternoon".

I was on my way home from work when two men with pistols in their hands opened fire on me out of the blue. A bullet hit me in the head. It was the businessman Sadik Yohedian who killed me".

The most famous parapsychologist in India, Dr. Chateda, examined the child and then ordered that the bones of the murder victim be exhumed for testing as well.

Two bullet holes were located in the skull of the murdered man. As it entered, the bullet made a hole approximately one centimeter above the right temple, exiting on the left side of the skull where the ear had been.

In comparison, X-rays performed on the child revealed a large crack in the skull from the right temple leading around to the area around the left ear.

Professor Chateda introduced the boy to the wife of the slain merchant. Tito told her about a picnic that he and the woman had enjoyed together during which he had given her a large box of sweets.

Only the wife and the husband had known about the picnic. Not only were they the only people to participate in it, but they had not mentioned it to anyone else at all.

The strangest thing of all: The Agra police arrested business man Yohedian based on the child's testimony. After a short period of interrogation, he admitted to the crime.

In another amazing account, which was reported in the Israeli press, a Druze-Israeli soldier fulfilling his service requirements with the Israel Defense Force claimed that he was the reincarnation of a Syrian soldier killed in a previous war.

He refused to continue serving in the army because of his inner conflict of having a reincarnated soul from an enemy army, as opposed to his desire to serve his own country.

A group of experts from the Israeli army carefully examined the soldier's circumstances in order to verify that his complaint was legitimate, and not some clever attempt to avoid his military obligation.

The soldier offered exact details about his place of birth in his previous life, a small village in Syria which he had never visited in his current incarnation.

The army experts confirmed the soldier's claim and he was released from his service due to his "past".

CHAPTER FOUR

Evil Spirits—Dibbukim

What is the meaning of the word *dibbukin*?

The word *dibbuk* in Hebrew, the singular form of *dibbukim* (Plural), means evil Spirit. Specifically, an evil spirit that enters and possesses the body of a living human being. In English, we know it as possession.

You may have heard of exorcism, when a Rabbi or a Priest is called to expel a spirit that invaded the body of a living human being.

A *dibbuk* is a paranormal phenomenon, and as such, it goes beyond the limit of our rational thinking. Therefore, it cannot be observed or explained scientifically. In the past however, centuries ago, it was a very common phenomenon in some cultures in various parts of the world such as Japan, India, Europe, the Far East and even the USA.

Because of its metaphysical nature, many people were not intimately familiar with all its details. Regardless of their ignorance on the subject, they were very curious about it, were aware of the fact that spiritual entities exist, and accepted it.

In nowadays, we have become more of a materialistic society, and therefore, the emphasis is on materialism of which science is a part of.

Many people doubt anything spiritual, and ridicule the whole topic due to its spiritual, intangible and unscientific nature.

However, the *Kabbalah* (Hebrew—Jewish esoteric thought), discusses it at length.

It begins by understanding what happens to the human being after he or she dies. It is not a simple matter.

The *Kabbalah* elaborates further by stating that death is not the cessation of all existence. Indeed, it is not the cessation of any existence. Death is the cessation of the physical existence, as we know it to be, where the physical body decays in the grave, and the soul, the essence of the human being, departs from this realm and goes into another dimension.

The soul lives on.

CHAPTER FIVE

What happens to the soul when we die?

What happens to the soul when we die?

There are various stages that the soul needs to go through before it gets to its final resting place. It could be a long journey, depending on several factors.

The *Kabbalah* elaborates and explains at length, the stages the soul experiences before it reaches its final resting place.

Most people are accustomed to believing that there are only two directions for the soul to go after the body dies—Heaven and Hell— Either Heaven or Hell. They don't realize that there is an in between realm called in Hebrew *Kaf Hakelaa*, which literally translates into English to *Sling Shot*.

Why is it called *Sling Shot*?

Because the soul in a way is being thrown from one end of the world to the other end. This soul is being pursued by certain malevolent angelic beings, certain demons as well, and cannot rest in peace while being in that realm.

Before we get into a deeper understanding of why the soul doesn't have any peace, we need to understand what happens immediately after we die.

The *Kabbalah* tells us that there is a judgment after we die, and that we are accountable for our deeds while we live in this world. Life requires certain responsibilities, and we are not merely here, on this earth for a ride, or to play golf. We are here on earth to fulfill a mission. Each and every one of us has a specific mission.

We are all human beings, created in the image of God—meaning that each one of us is special and is here for a purpose.

Transgressions will lead to tribulations in life—not as punishment, but to stimulate soul searching and to help us make the right choice—for the ultimate and eternal benefit of our soul.

All of us should remember that we are mere mortals. Here today, gone tomorrow.

Let us review the stages of our soul's journey after we die, after the funeral, burial and the like.

According to the *Zohar* (Hebrew—Book of splendor, radiance the 2nd Century C.E. esoteric interpretation of the Torah by Rabbi Shimon Bar Yochai and his disciples), there are seven judgments.

1. The first judgment, as the soul departs the body, is the judgment of someone's deeds. Everything that has been done or said by the individual has been recorded.

2. As he or she is being led to be buried, the second judgment occurs. All of the individual's deeds—good or bad—are being called out.

3. As he or she is being put into the grave, yet the third judgment occurs, describing what he or she has done.

4. When the body is in the grave, the fourth stage is in motion, which is called by the *Kabbalah: Chivut Hakever* (Beating of the grave).

5. The fifth judgment is the judgment of the corpse itself. As it is consumed by worms (which is also painful even though the physical body no longer feels the pain because it's dead),the soul is pained to see how the body is being decomposed. The soul's pain lasts until the body decays.

6. The sixth stage is called in Hebrew *Gehenom* (Temporary Hell)—if that applies.

7. The last stage is called in Hebrew *Kaf Hakelaa* (the *Sling Shot)*—if that applies.

What is the sling shot?

What is the *Sling Shot*? What is so unique about it?

The majority of people think that Hell is the worst final destination to go to after we die. In reality, it is not. What Hell is, metaphorically speaking, is a very hot shower. It is a lot more magnified than the hot showers we are familiar with.

According to *Kabbalah*, there are various levels of burning in Hell, various departments for different lengths of time. However, the worst of judgments according to *Kabbalah* is the *Sling Shot*, because it can go on for centuries at times. Being in that realm means that the soul has no rest—a wandering soul—

It is so horrible that the soul must have done something so terribly wrong in its lifetime that it is not given permission to enter Hell.

Only after completing the *Sling Shot* phase would they allow this soul to go to Hell. And only after completing the Hell phase, would the Heavenly Judges allow that soul to be reincarnated.

Reincarnation is the easiest phase of all, because one can come back and live a comfortable life. However, that soul has to go through all the stages of being born, being a child, an adult and so on.

Reincarnation is a *tikkun* (Hebrew—correction) of the soul, by being given a second chance (or more) to correct the wrongs done in a previous life, or to accomplish what is lacking and needed to be accomplished in a previous lifetime.

The soul meanwhile is wandering in the *Sling Shot* phase without any rest, and is being pursued by demons and malevolent angelic beings. It is a very painful experience for that soul because it is constant and without rest, except on the Sabbath.

This entity at times is allowed to enter a human being—a man, woman or child—to possess them and live within them. At the moment they enter another human's body, they have some sort of physical rest from the demons and malevolent angels that are pursuing them.

Although not being their ultimate resting place, it is better than being constantly pursued. Their possession of a human body is for a limited time only.

The reason it is called a *dibbuk* in Hebrew is because the moment they enter a human body, it is in partial control of that body. The possessed person has almost no control, except for certain times during the day or night, when it acts "normal", when it acts as itself. When the *dibbuk* acts up, the possessed human being loses control.

CHAPTER SIX

How can we detect a possession?

How can we detect the possession of a human being by a *dibbuk*?

We may not know with 100% certainty, but there are various symptoms that will point to it.

One of them is that a possessed person will all of a sudden experience seizures, similar to epileptic seizures, although they never had a medical history of seizures or epilepsy prior to their possession.

Another clue will be that unusual swelling will occur in the possessed body, in different parts of his or her body. First the arm will swell up, then the leg, then the thighs etc. The swelling will move from one part of the body to another.

Another symptom could be, that the possessed will feel as if they are being strangled. Their eyes will roll from time to time.

The strongest symptom that will unequivocally certify that it is indeed a possession, is when a strange voice, not belonging to the possessed person, will come out and originate not from the possessed mouth, but from his or her stomach. The tongue barely moves, which indicates that the vocal chords are not doing the talking. The voice heard comes from the stomach, and in some cases, you may see the possessed person's stomach move up and down.

This has been observed in many cultures throughout history.

What are these *dibbukim* trying to accomplish by invading a body other than getting some rest from the pursuing angels?

They are searching for a *tikkun*, correction for their souls. They need someone to help them. They are stuck in the *Sling Shot* phase perhaps for many years, and they simply need help.

Those of us who left this world cannot do anything to help themselves anymore, and they depend on those who are still alive to help them make their soul correction.

How can they invade a human body?

They were given permission to do so by those who are appointed over them. The possessed individual also must have done something to deserve being possessed, otherwise the possessing entity would not have gotten the permission to invade their body, and cause them so much pain.

Many *dibbukim* remain anonymous. They prefer to keep a low profile and barely hurt the possessed body. They just don't want to be exorcised.

Who can exorcise a possessed body?

Only the utmost righteous kabbalists rabbis would attempt to do it due to the dangerous risks involved in the process. The possessing entity can harm people who are present in the room. Usually, those rabbis who attempted exorcism knew exactly what they were doing.

What becomes evident to all witnesses of a performed exorcism, is the knowledge and certainty that there is a Judge and there is Judgment: there is reward and punishment. Any non-believer and skeptical person who witnessed an exorcism being performed came out of the room all shaken and knowing that death is not a finality.

There is something after death, and we are accountable for our actions while we are still alive.

Without a post-physical world, a grand scheme of reward and punishment is superfluous.

We all know or have heard of people who have mental problems and are emotionally disturbed, are institutionalized, and some diagnosed as extremely schizophrenic.

Since many *dibbukim* remain anonymous, there is a possibility that some of these patients haven't been properly diagnosed, and that a *dibbuk* invaded their body.

Physicians who do not believe in the paranormal realm could never reach this conclusion. Many illnesses are not really illnesses but indicative of a *dibbuk's* presence.

There is a reference book, *Minchat Yehuda,* written in Hebrew and Arabic in the beginning of the 20th century by the holy Chief Rabbi of Baghdad, Irak, amongst the greatest of the kabbalists of recent generations, Rabbi Yehudah Fatayah (1859-1942).

In his book, the Rabbi describes his encounters with such *dibbukim* first hand, how he has helped them with their soul correction, and how the *dibbukim* tell him in details what happens in the afterlife.

Our powers of comprehension and cognizance become greatly enhanced when we realize that our lives began long before we're born and continue long after we die.

Here are some of the testimonies told by Rabbi Yehudah Fatayah in his book, *Minchat Yehudah*:

"In the year 1907, after returning from the holy city of Jerusalem (to Baghdad, where he lived) a woman named Rimah bat Pharchah came to me, and she had within her a spirit named Yitzchak ben Katoon, an evil promiscuous man who was a complete boor. I battled with it for several years but it didn't come out. It remains within Rimah until today, 1933, having blinded her in both eyes, may the Merciful One save us".

CHAPTER SEVEN

Ephraim the *dibbuk*

Note: the following true account told by Rabbi Yehudah Fetayah may be disturbing to some readers. The purpose of sharing it with you, in all its details, is mainly to reinforce the fact that we are all accountable for our actions in this world, and that there is Judgment and a Judge after we die.

"In the year 1911, in the month of Elul (12th month of the Hebrew calendar), a spirit entered into a young man named Ephraim ben Nissim Changil, and afflicted him greatly. His mother and father asked a Muslim spiritualist for assistance, but it didn't help.

The spirit demanded: "Have mercy on me and bring me Yehudah (i.e. Rabbi Yehudah Fetayah) and I will listen to everything that he tells me, because he will rectify me". His mother and father and all of his relatives came to me.

When I came to his house, I found him lying on the bed, his eye rolling into the back of his head, deranged with the spirit speaking from his throat.

I said to the spirit: "What is your name?" It did not want to give its name. After I performed several Kabbalistic meditations, it said that its name was Ephraim ben Avad Netzer Allah (basic Arabic translation: "God will protect"). His mother was Esther and they used to live in our

41

neighborhood (in the house in which I live now). He never married and died at the age of forty.

The reason for his return to this world was because of the fact that he had been a mule driver, who delivered goods to the villages in the region.

Once he drove a woman with a large caravan to the grave of Ezekiel the Prophet (buried in Irak). He trailed behind the caravan, then led her a different way, threatened to kill her if she screamed and raped her.

Another time, he accompanied a caravan in the desert and had relations with his donkey. Also, on the holy Sabbath, he had forbidden relations with a man in the orchard of the village of Bakuba.

A few years later, he had a dispute with some Muslim mule drivers, and while he was delivering the goods to the village of Bakuba, they ganged up on him and killed him, and left him in an unmarked grave. They abandoned everything including his mule and his gear on the trail.

His brother Saul went looking for him, took what had been left behind, did not return the goods to their rightful owners, and did not look for the body. He took all of his brother's money and possessions from his house and did not pay back his creditors anything.

He also neglected to provide any of the comforts for the dead traditionally performed during the twelve months after death (*Kaddish,* mourning customs, etc.). And because the spirit greatly suffered from this, he caused his brother to make many mistakes, until he lost all of his wealth and eventually died disgracefully after a difficult illness.

And know that in the place where I am buried, there are other Jews buried as well. It has been seventeen years since I was killed.

I asked the spirit whether he had repented at the time he was killed. He replied that he had been very scared, and it never even occurred to him to repent, especially since he was an ignorant who didn't even think about repenting. He didn't wear *tzitzit* or even put on *tefillin* more than three times in his life. He didn't pray either—except on *Yom Kippur*.

The spirit of Ephraim continued: "But that was not my first incarnation in the world.

My start in the world came as a certain native of *Tzefat* (Safed—northern town in Israel) by the name of Shlomo ben Yechezkel. But because I sinned a great deal, it was decreed that I go through a series of reincarnations, from mineral, vegetable, animal to human.

I wound up as a pomegranate and an old, pious man named Shimon purchased it. He ate the fruit at a Sabbath meal, reciting two blessings on it, and in this way I was rectified.

Then I would up in the city of Izmir (Turkey), as a man named Chayim. (He was not required to be reincarnated as an animal, as originally decreed, since the old man Shimon raised him up two levels—from plant to human).

This is explained in the introduction to the book *Sha'ar Ha-Gilgulim*—Gate of reincarnation). But that man was fond of eating *chelev* (forbidden non-kosher animal fat) because he has heard from ignorant people that it was good for his health. And at the end of his days he went up to Jerusalem and there he passed away.

Afterwards, the soul was born into me, Ephraim of Babylon (Irak), and I didn't rectify it at all. Rather, I sinned and blemished it even more.

From the time of the death of Shlomo, mentioned above (his first incarnation), until this day, about four hundred and fifty years have passed, and during that entire time, my soul wandered from place to place in this way.

After I died, thirty five destroying angels came to hit me for fifteen hours a day. The other nine hours a day, they would take me into the desert, full of snakes and scorpions that would bite at and eat my skin, and then I would return to life. This process continued for four years.

Afterward, they judged me in *Gehenom* (a temporary hell) fifteen hours a day, and for the remaining nine hours, they lowered me into a deep, dark pit, covered it with a large boulder, and stood on top of it. And this process continued for a long time until they gave permission for me to enter this boy, because he has sinned as a child.

When he was a little boy, he went with his father to the village of Bakuba. On that Sabbath, in that same orchard where I had had relations with the man mentioned before, he tore a branch from the very same tree under which we had been. However, they did not give me permission to enter into the boy, since he was small. Now, I was able to gain control over him for a different reason, and they gave me permission to enter into him.

I came into him in the evening, when he was arguing with his mother about dinner. I entered through the top of his head and he felt a pain like a thick needle entering his skull, and I started to torture him, just as you see. And now I request from your Honor to rectify me spiritually, for God's sake"

I asked the spirit if he had heard or seen or knew of the fate of Nathan of Gaza (a disciple of Shabttai Zevi), and whether he had already gone to *Gehenom*, or if his soul was still in the "sling".

He said: "I haven't seen it with my own eyes, but during the nine months I was in the pit, I once heard loud voices like that of a wedding celebration, and I asked the ones in charge of me what was all the noise. They told me that Nathan of Gaza's punishment in the "Sling" has ended, and that he was now being sent to *Gehenom*".

During this conversation, his mother brought (the boy) some meat to eat. When he took a piece to eat, he said to those sitting around him: "Look how in this piece is the soul of an eighty seven year old woman, who was punished for combing her hair in the courtyard next to an open door, leading to the street. (Even though she had always covered her hair, as required by Jewish law, she had not been careful about combing it in a way that a passerby shouldn't see it, and this is why she was punished with reincarnation).

Even the piece of pomegranate in the other bowl contains the soul of a girl. Even the bird that sits on a branch of a tree on the right contains the spirit of a girl who lived for only three days. I see all of this with my eyes and I can't believe that none of you see this. Therefore, one of you must make a blessing on these pieces (of food) with concentration, and all of the rest of you must answer "amen" in order to repair the souls spiritually". We did according to his request.

I said to the spirit: "would you prefer to leave this body completely and smoothly, or shall it be by force and with shame? Because no matter what, you need to leave today. And if you refuse, I will send you out against your will by means of holy names and oaths". He said to me: "Yes, I will do as you say because I also want to leave. However, I will not leave until 12:20pm—the time I came in". I said to him: "That is impossible, for today is the eve of both the Sabbath and Rosh Hashanah. We need to prepare ourselves for both of them, and we cannot be delayed by you. Better for you to get out now, when souls are ascending to the Garden of Eden, in order that you too join them". The spirit answered: "All of Sabbath is holy and I can rise up at the moment of my own choosing".

Then I started to force him out through *yichudim* (kabbalistic meditations). He screamed in a bitter voice and said: "If this is the case then I will leave at 11:30 today". I said to him: "I don't accept that either. You must leave now". He said to me: "If this is the case, go buy your things for the Sabbath and come back to me at the eighth hour. May God have mercy on us and we'll see what we can do".

I said to him: "Alright, but you must not trouble Ephraim until I return to deal with you". He agreed.

I returned at eight and started performing *yichudim*, and blew twelve *shofar* blasts near his ear. The spirit rose up and screamed: "I want to leave without being forced! ". I said to him: "From which body part do you want to leave?". He said: "His eyes". I scolded him that he not leave from his eyes because that would blind him. "Fine" he said. "Then I will leave from his mouth". I reproached him again. Then he said he would leave from his teeth, but promised to knock out only the particular premolar from which he would exit. I rejected this too.

So he asked me: "Then from which body part do you want me to go out of?". I said to him: "From the small toe of his left foot between the nail and the skin". He told me that it was a big problem for him to leave from the end of the body because it is the place to which ritually impure elements cling.

I forced him with more *yichudim*, oaths and threats of eternal excommunication that he would leave only through the small toe of the left foot, without damaging any other part of the body—even that same little toe from which he must get out. And I made him promise that he would never again enter into or harm any other human being.

He became very angry and said: "How can I not tear away or at least damage the little toe from which I will leave?"

I was forced to speak to him more gently so that he would not get upset and begin to hurt him (the young man). "It seems as if you have a very big soul, and it is only due to your sins that you had to be reincarnated. Actually, you are humble and shy. You love the Torah and respect rabbis. Because of this, I do not want this young man to be hurt at all, so that you are not counted among the souls of the wicked who are the scourge of the world (*Zohar* 2:118), or be considered like one of them".

Then, the spirit surrendered and replied: "Your words are very good and true. I am ready to force myself, and overcome my initial desire, so that I don't hurt him at all. Nevertheless, he will still remain ill for another fifteen days and then he will become well".

I said to him: "That simply cannot be. These are the most precious days of the year, and there are many Biblical commandments associated with them: From Rosh Hashanah, Sabbath, hearing of the *shofar*, the Ten Days of Repentance, *Yom Kippur*, *Sukkah*, *lulav* and *etrog*, *Hoshanah Rabbah* and the completion of the Torah reading. You are going to prevent him from doing all of those commandments! And also from the commandments of *tzitzit* and *tefillin*, and from the obligation of prayer. This will really hurt you in the realm of souls". He said: "But the greatest pain is mine, if I don't do anything bad to him". I said to him: "It is appropriate for you to go through this pain for the sake of the Holy One and for the sake of His commandments". The spirit said: "Woe is me, if I do as you say. Still I must suffer all of this for God's sake".

And then in the midst of this, the spirit added: "The tenth hour is coming. I want to go. I now request that you begin studying so that my spirit will leave amidst words of Torah, so I might be rectified".

I began studying the verses: "May the Lord answer you on the day of distress . . . (Psalms 20:2), and "He who dwells in the secret place of the Most High . . . (ibid. 91:1), and "When I call, answer me . . . (ibid. 4:2), and acrostics of the initials of Ephraim ben Esther (from Psalms 119), and "The tale of iniquities is too heavy for me . . . (ibid. 65:4), and Ezekiel's chariot and "What God is like you . . . ." (Michah 7:18), and the *Idra Rabbah* from "Rabbi Shimon opened and said . . ." to the end of the thirteen attributes, the *Zohar* on the Torah portion *Vayakhel* (p.219b), from "Rabbi Shimon and Rabbi Elazar were sitting" to "Arise and sing, you dwellers in the dust", the incense offering, *Shemah Israel* and *Anna b'ko'ach,* and then I said "May it be your will . . . ." as quoted previously in Isaiah 30.

"As you study" said the spirit," I am going out". He said "*Shalom Aleichem*—Goodbye!" and went out from the boy, as he had promised, without inflicting any further harm.

Immediately the boy sat up and returned to his senses, for he hadn't felt anything that happened to him. Though he wondered why there was a group of men and women standing around him and why his mother and father were crying. The people said to him that it was nothing, that he had fainted a bit and they had come to visit him.

Then everyone left right away, each to his own business. His father and mother kissed him.

I said to them: "Thank God nothing bad happened to him. I already ordered a protective amulet for him to wear after the spirit departed, according to the custom of *Arizal*".

Likewise, the spirit said before he left that the ones appointed over him had said that Ephraim must wear an amulet around his neck on which are written the four Names of God known to me.

However, I suspected that the spirit never really left the boy, but rather cleverly hid itself in his body. The afflicted child had not made a single movement of his body or feet, as usually happens. Still I ignored it and pretended that I was convinced that the spirit was completely gone.

Night was coming and it was time to go to synagogue. I also wanted to trick the spirit into thinking that we believed that he had already left, so that he would carefully stay out of sight and not bother the young man for at least the two days of Rosh Hashanah. After that, God would have mercy on us.

And so it was that after the two days of Rosh Hashanah, the boy slowly became sicker and sicker, until the spirit revealed itself on the Sabbath between *Rosh Hashanah* and *Yom Kippur*, and caused the boy to faint.

On the Saturday night, the eve of *Yom Kippur*, I went and said to him: "You are a liar. You promised that you would already be gone on *Rosh Hashanah*, but you were hiding in the boy's body".

He told me that he had already left on *Rosh Hashanah*, but because he had gone out before the exact time he had entered, he had been forced to return again. (This idea was ridiculous!) He said he was ready and willing to leave at the end of *Yom Kippur* and requested that the father of the boy circle four chickens over the head of his son and then slaughter them (a custom called *kaparot*, performed on the eve of *Yom Kippur*).

The spirit did not want there to be less than four chickens, and he also did not want to explain why. Perhaps he wanted one chicken for each of his incarnations, plus one for the boy.

When they brought the four chickens in front of him, he grabbed them in his hand and said: "In this chicken is one incarnated soul!" Then he turned to me and begged me to slaughter it, with the appropriate blessing (for I have been a certified slaughterer since 1882). I did as I was asked and the spirit did as he said he would.

Near the end of *Yom Kippur*, the boy Ephraim went to the synagogue where he always prayed, and according to people who prayed there, the boy fainted during the closing prayers of the service.

The spirit screamed at the worshippers that they must leave the synagogue. Some of the people left and some did not because they wanted to see what would happen.

The spirit said to them that if they didn't move away from him, he would publicly reveal each and everyone of their sins.

Then everyone moved away. (Actually he was worried about hurting them when he came out). He yelled at the *shofar* blower and told him to have him in mind when he blows the *shofar* (at the conclusion of the service).

When the *shofar* was blown, he told the people that the archangel appointed over the prayers and *shofar* blows of all of Israel has descended to collect them—and that the spirit was going to leave with him and ascend to the Garden of Eden. The boy screamed out loudly from the terrible pain in his leg, and pounded his left foot on the floor with great force. Then the spirit left altogether and the boy sat peacefully, whole in both body and mind. He could not walk because of the pain in his leg and they carried him home. By morning, he was healthy again.

CHAPTER EIGHT

Who were Shabttai Zevi and Nathan of Gaza?

Who were Shabttai Zevi and Nathan of Gaza mentioned in this story?

Shabttai Zevi

Shabttai Zevi was born in Smyrna, Turkey, on (supposedly) 9th Av 1626 (a Sabbath), and died, according to some, on Yom Kippur, September 30, 1676, in Dulcigno, a small town in the coastal region of Montenegro, now called Ulcinj. Zevi's family were Romaniotes from Patras; his father, Mordecai, was a poor poultry dealer in the Morea.

Later, when in consequence of the war between Turkey and Venice under the Sultan Ibrahim I, Smyrna became the center of Levantine trade, Mordecai became the Smyrnan agent of an English house. As a consequence, he acquired considerable wealth.

Shabttai Zevi early years

In accordance with the prevailing Jewish custom, Shabttai's father had him study the Talmud. In his early youth he attended a *yeshiva* under the rabbi of Smyrna, Joseph Escapa. Studies in *halachah* (Jewish law) did not appeal to him, but apparently he did attain proficiency in the Talmud at an early age. On the other hand, he was fascinated by mysticism and the *Kabbalah*, in the prevailing style of Rabbi Isaac Luria.

He found the practical *Kabbalah*, with its asceticism, and its mortification of the body—through which its devotees claimed to be able to communicate with God and the angels, to predict the future and to perform all sorts of miracles—especially appealing.

In his youth he was inclined to solitude. According to custom he married early, but he avoided intercourse with his wife; she therefore applied for a divorce, which he willingly granted. The same thing happened with a second wife. When he was about twenty years of age, he began to develop unusual behaviors. He would alternately sink into deep depression and isolation, and become filled with frenzied restlessness and ecstasy. He felt compelled to eat non kosher food, speak the forbidden name of God, and commit other "holy sins".

Influence of English millenarianism

During the first half of the 17th century, millenarian ideas of the approach of the Messianic time, and more especially of the redemption of the Jews and their return to the land of Israel, with their own independent sovereignty, were popular.

The apocalyptic year was identified by Christian authors as 1666. This belief was so dominant that Manasseh ben Israel, in his letter to Oliver Cromwell and the Rump Parliament, did not hesitate to use it for his plea for the readmission of the Jews into England (since their expulsion in 1210), remarking "the opinion of many Christians and mine do concur herein, that we both believe that the restoring time of our Nation into their native country is very near at hand".

Shabttai's father, who as the agent of an English house was in constant touch with English people, must frequently have heard of these expectations and, being strongly inclined to believe them, must have communicated them to his son, whom he almost deified because of his piety and kabbalistic wisdom.

Claims of messiahship

Apart from this general Messianic theory, there was another computation, based on an interpreted passage in the *Zohar*, and particularly popular among the Jews, according to which the year 1648 was to be the year of Israel's redemption by their long-awaited Jewish Messiah.

Though only twenty-two years old, Shabttai chose (in the year 1648) to reveal himself at Smyrna to a group of followers as the true Messianic redeemer, designated by God to overthrow the governments of the nations and to restore the kingdom of Israel.

His mode of revealing his mission was the pronouncing of the Tetragrammaton in Hebrew, an act which Judaism emphatically prohibited, except the Jewish high priest in the Temple in Jerusalem on the day of atonement.

This was of great significance to those acquainted with rabbinical, and especially kabbalistic literature.

However, Shabttai's authority at the age of twenty-two did not reach far enough for him to gain many adherents.

Among the first of those to whom he revealed his Messiahship were: Isaac Silveyra and Moses Pinheiro, the latter a brother-in-law of the Italian rabbi and kabbalist Joseph Ergas.

Shabttai remained at Smyrna for several years, leading the pious life of a mystic, and giving rise to much argument in the community, the details of which are not known. The college of rabbis, having at its head his teacher, Joseph Escapa, watched Shabttai closely, and when his Messianic pretensions became too bold they put him and his followers under a ban of *cherem*, a type of excommunication in classical Judaism.

About the year 1651 (according to others, 1654) Shabttai and his disciples were banished from Smyrna. It is not quite certain where he went from there. In 1653, or at the latest 1658, he was in Constantinople, where he met a preacher, Abraham ha-Yakini, a disciple of Joseph di Trani, who confirmed Shabttai.

Ha-Yakini is said to have forged a manuscript in archaic characters and in a style imitating the ancient apocalypses, and which, he alleged, bore testimony to Shabttai's Messiahship. It was entitled *The Great Wisdom of Salomon*, and began:

"I, Abraham, was confined in a cave for forty years, and I wondered greatly that the time of miracles did not arrived. Then was heard a voice proclaiming, "A son will be born in the Hebrew year 5386 (English calendar year 1626) to Mordecai Zevi; and he will be called Shabttai. He will humble the great dragon . . . he, the true Messiah, will sit upon My throne".

In Salonica

With this document, which he appears to have accepted as an actual revelation, Shabttai determined to choose Salonica, at that time a center of kabbalists, as the field for his further operations.

Here he boldly proclaimed himself the Messiah, gaining many adherents. In order to impress his Messiahship upon the minds of his enthusiastic friends he put on all sorts of mystical events—e.g., the celebration of his marriage to the "One Without End" (*the Ein Sof*) with the Torah, preparing a solemn festival to which he invited his friends.

The consequence was that the rabbis of Salonica, headed by Rabbi Hiyya Abraham Di Boton, banished him from the city.

The sources differ widely as to the route he took after this expulsion, Alexandria, Athens, Constantinople, Jerusalem, Smyrna and other places being mentioned as temporary centers.

Finally, however, after long wanderings, he settled in Cairo, where he resided for about two years (1660-1662).

At that time there lived in Cairo a very wealthy and influential Jew named Raphael Joseph Halabi, who held the high position of mint-master and tax-farmer under the Ottoman government.

Despite his riches and the external splendor which he displayed before the public, he continued to lead privately an ascetic life, fasting, bathing, and frequently scourging his body at night.

He used his great wealth benevolently, supplying the needs of poor Talmudists and Kabbalists, fifty of whom regularly dined at his table. Shabttai at once made the acquaintance of Raphael Joseph, who became one of the most zealous promulgators of his Messianic claims.

He left the Egyptian capital and traveled to Jerusalem. Arriving there in about 1663, he at first remained inactive, so as not to offend the community. He resumed his former practice of mortifying the body by frequent fasting and other penances. Many saw this as proof of his extraordinary piety.

Having a very melodious voice, he sang psalms for the whole night, or at times even coarse Spanish love-songs, to which he gave mystical interpretations, thus attracting crowds of admiring listeners.

At other times he would pray at the graves of pious men and women and, some of his followers reported, shed flood of tears. He distributed all sorts of sweetmeats to the children on the streets. Thus he gradually gathered around him a circle of adherents who placed their faith in him.

At this point an unexpected incident took him back to Cairo. The community of Jerusalem needed money in order to avert a calamity which Turkish officials planned against it.

Shabttai, known as the favorite of the rich Raphael Joseph Halabi, was chosen as the envoy of the distressed community, and he willingly undertook the task, as it gave him an opportunity to act as the deliverer of the Holy City. As soon as he appeared before Halabi, he obtained from him the necessary sum, which gave him great prestige. His worshipers dated his public career from this second journey to Cairo.

Marriage to Sarah

Another circumstance assisted Shabttai in the course of his second stay at Cairo. During the Chmielnicki massacres in Poland, a Jewish orphan girl named Sarah, about six years old, had been found by Christians and sent to a convent.

After ten years' confinement she escaped and was taken to Amsterdam. Some years later she went to Livorno where, according to authentic reports, she led a life of prostitution. She also conceived the notion that she was to become the bride of the Messiah who was soon to appear. The report of this girl reached Cairo, and Shabttai claimed that such a consort had been promised to him in a dream because he, as the Messiah, was bound to fall in love with an unchaste woman . . . Messengers were sent to Livorno, and Sarah was brought to Cairo, where she was married to Shabttai at Halabi's house.

Through her, a romantic licentious element entered Shabttai's career. Her beauty and eccentricity gained for him many new followers, and even her past lewd life was looked upon as an additional confirmation of his Messiahship, the prophet Hosea having commanded to take a "wife of whoredom" as the first symbolic act of his calling.

Nathan of Gaza

Having Halabi's money, a charming wife, and many additional followers, Shabttai triumphantly returned to Palestine.

Passing through the city of Gaza, he met a man who was to become very active in his subsequent Messianic career. This was Nathan Benjamin Levi, known under the name of Nathan of Gaza.

He became Shabttai's right-hand man and professed to be the risen Elijah, the precursor of the Messiah.

In 1665, Nathan announced that the Messianic age was to begin in the following year. Shabttai spread this announcement widely, together with many additional details to the effect that the world would be conquered by him, the Elijah, without bloodshed; that the Messiah would then lead back the Ten Lost Tribes to the Holy Land, "riding on a lion with a seven-headed dragon in its jaws". These claims were widely circulated and believed.

The rabbis of Jerusalem regarded the movement with great suspicion, and threatened its followers with excommunication.

Shabttai, realizing that Jerusalem was not a congenial place in which to carry out his plans, left for his native city Smyrna, while his prophet, Nathan, proclaimed that henceforth Gaza, and not Jerusalem, would be the sacred city.

On his way from Jerusalem to Smyrna, Shabttai was enthusiastically greeted in the large Asiatic community of Aleppo, and at Smyrna, which he reached in the autumn of 1665, the greatest homage was paid to him.

Finally, after some hesitation, he publicly declared himself as the expected Messiah, on the Jewish New Year of 1665.

The declaration was made in the synagogue, with the blowing of the *shofar*, and the multitude greeted him with: "Long live our King, our Messiah!"

Proclaimed Messiah

The joy of his followers knew no bounds. Shabttai, assited by his wife, now became the sole ruler of the community. In this capacity, he used his power to crush all opposition. For instance, he deposed the old rabbi of Smyrna, Aaron Lapapa, and appointed in his place Hayyim Benveniste.

His popularity grew with incredible rapidity, as not only Jews but Christians also spread and accepted his story far and wide.

His fame extendend to all countries. Italy, Germany, and the Netherlands had centers where the Messianic movement was ardently promulgated, and the Jews of Hamburg and Amsterdam received confirmation of the extraordinary events in Smyrna from trustworthy Christians.

A distinguished German savant, Heinrich Oldenburg, wrote to Baruch Spinoza: "All the world here is talking of a rumor of the return of the Israelites . . . to their own country . . . . Should the news be confirmed, it may bring about a revolution in all things".

Shabttai numbered many prominent rabbis as followers, including Isaac Aboab da Fonseca, Moses Raphael de Aguilar, Moses Galante, Moses Zacuto, and the above-mentioned Hayyim Benveniste.

Even the semi-Spinozist Dionysius Mussafia Musaphia likewise became one of Shabttai's zealous adherents.

Fantastic reports were widely spread and believed, as for example: "in the north of Scotland a ship had appeared with silken sails and ropes, manned by sailors who spoke Hebrew. The flag bore the inscription "The Twelve Tribes of Israel". The community of Avignon, France, prepared to emigrate to the new kingdom in the spring of 1666.

The readiness of the Jews of the time to believe the messianic claims of Shabttai Zevi may be largely explained by the desperate state of European Jewry in the mid-1600's.

The bloody pogroms of Bodhan Khmelnytsky had wiped out one third of the Jewish population and destroyed many centers of Jewish learning and communal life. There is no doubt that for most of the Jews of Europe there could never have seemed a more propitious moment for the messiah to deliver salvation than the moment at which Shabttai Zevi made his appearance.

Spread of his influence

The adherents of Shabttai, probably with his consent, even planned to abolish to a great extent the ritualistic observances because, according to a minority opinion in the Talmud, in the Messianic time, most of them were to lose their obligatory character.

The first step toward the desintegration of traditional Judaism was the changing of the fast of the Tenth of Tevet to a day of feasting and rejoicing. Samuel Primo, a man who entered Shabttai's service as secretary at the time when the latter left Jerusalem for Smyrna, directed in the name of the Messiah the following circular to the whole of Israel:

"The first-begotten Son of God, Shabttai Zevi, Messiah and Redeemer of the people of Israel, to all the sons of Israel, Peace! Since ye have been deemed worthy to behold the great day and the fulfilment of God's word by the Prophets, your lament and sorrow must be changed into joy, and your fasting into merriment; for ye shall weep no more. Rejoice with song and melody, and change the day formerly spent in sadness and sorrow into a day of jubilee, because I have appeared".

The message produced wild excitement and dissension in the communities, as many of the leaders, who had hitherto regarded the movement as sympathetically, were shocked at these radical innovations.

Salomon Algazi, a prominent Talmudist of Smyrna, and other members of the rabbinate, who opposed the abolition of the fast, narrowly escaped with their lives.

In Istanbul

At the beginning of the year 1666, Shabttai again left Smyrna for Istanbul, the Ottoman Empire's capital, which was still known in the Christian West at the time as Constantinople, either because he was compelled to do so by the city authorities or because of a hope that a miracle would happen in the Turkish capital to fulfill the prophecy of Nathan of Gaza, that Shabttai would place the sultan's crown on his own head.

As soon as he reached the landing-place, however, he was arrested at the command of the grand vizier, Ahmed Koprulu, and cast into prison in chains.

Shabttai's imprisonment had no discouraging effect either on him or on his followers. On the contrary, the lenient treatment which he secured by means of bribes served rather to strengthen them in their Messianic delusions.

In the meantime, all sorts of fabulous reports concerning the miraculous deeds which "the Messiah" was performing in the Turkish capital were spread by Nathan of Gaza and Primo among the Jews of Smyrna and in many other communities, and the expectations of the Jews were raised to a still higher pitch.

At Abydos (*Migdal Oz*)

After two months' imprisonment in Constantinople, Shabttai was brought to the state prison in the castle of Abydos.

Here he was treated very leniently, some of his friends even being allowed to accompany him. In consequence, the Shabttaians called that fortress *Migdal Oz* (Tower of Strength). As the day on which he was brought to Abydos was the day preceding Passover, he slew a paschal lamb for himself and his followers and ate it with its fat, which was a violation of the Law. It is said that he pronounced over it a benediction: "Blessed be God who hath restored again that which was forbidden".

The immense sums sent to him by his rich adherents, the charms of the queenly Sarah and the reverential admiration shown him even by the Turkish officials and the inhabitants of the place enabled Shabttai to display a royal splendor in the castle of Abydos, accounts of which were exaggerated and spread among Jews in Europe, Asia and Africa.

In some parts of Europe, Jews began to unroof their houses and prepare for a new "exodus".

In almost every synagogue, Shabttai's initials were posted, and prayers for him were inserted in the following form: "Bless our Lord and King, the holy and righteous Shabttai Zevi, the Messiah of the God of Jacob".

In Hamburg, the council introduced this custom of praying for Shabttai not only on Saturday, the Jewish Sabbath, but also on Monday and Thursday, and unbelievers were compelled to remain in the synagogue and join in the prayer with a loud *Amen*.

Shabttai's picture was printed together with that of king David in most of the prayer-books, as well as his kabbalistic formulas and penances.

These and similar innovations caused great dissension in various communities.

On Moravia, the excitement reached such a pitch that the government had to interfere, while at Sale, Morocco, the emir ordered a persecution of the Jews. It was during this period that Shabttai transformed the fasts of the Seventeenth of Tammuz and the Ninth of Av (his birthday) into feasts-days, and it is said that he contemplated even the abolition of the Day of Atonement.

Nehemiah Ha-Cohen

At this time, an incident occurred which led to the discrediting of Shabttai's Messiahship.

Two prominent Polish Talmudists from Lwow, Galicia, who were among Shabttai's visitors in Abydos, apprised him of the fact that in their native country a prophet, Nehemiah ha-Kohen had announced the coming of the Messiah.

Shabttai ordered the prophet to appear before him. Nehamiah obeyed, reaching Abydos, after a journey of three months, at the beginning of September, 1666.

The conference between the two ended in mutual dissatisfaction, and some fanatical Shabttaians are said to have contemplated the secret murder of the dangerous rival.

Shabttai adopts Islam

Nehemiah, however, escaped to Constantinople, where he pretended to embrace Islam to get an audience with the kaymakam and betrayed the treasonable desires of Shabttai to him. He in turn informed the sultan, Mehmed IV.

At the command of Mehmed, Shabttai was now taken from Abydos to Adrianople, where the sultan's physician, a former Jew, advised him to convert to Islam. Shabttai realized the danger of the situation and adopted the physician's advice.

On the following day, September 16, 1666, being brought before the sultan, he cast off his Jewish garb and put a Turkish turban on his head, and thus his conversion to Islam was accomplished. The sultan was much pleased, and rewarded Shabttai by conferring on him the title Mahmed *Effendi*, and appointing him as his doorkeeper with a high salary.

Sarah and a number of Shabttai's followers also went over to Islam.

To complete his acceptance of Islam, Shabttai was ordered to take an additional wife. Some days after his conversion, he wrote to Smyrna:

"God has made me an Ishmaelite; He commanded, and it was done. The ninth day of my regeneration".

Disillusion

Shabttai's conversion was devastating for his followers. In addition to the misery and disappointment from within, Muslims and Christians jeered at and scorned the credulous Jews.

In spite of Shabttai's apostasy, many of his adherents still tenaciously clung to him, claiming that his conversion was a part of the Messianic scheme. This belief was further upheld and strengthened by false prophets like Nathan of Gaza and Primo, who were interested in maintaining the movement.

In many communities the Seventeenth of Tammuz and the Ninth of Av were still observed as feasts-days in spite of bans and excommunications.

At times, Shabttai would assume the role of a pious Muslim and revile Judaism, at others, he would enter into relations with Jews as one of their own faith.

In March 1668, he announced again that he had been filled with the "Holy Spirit" at Passover, and had received a "revelation". He, or one of his followers, published a mystical work addressed to the Jews in which it was claimed that Shabttai was the true Messiah, in spite of his conversion, his object being to bring over thousands of Muslims to Judaism.

To the sultan, however, he said that his activity among the Jews was to bring them over to Islam. He therefore received permission to associate with his former co-religionists, and even to preach in their synagogues. He thus succeeded in bringing over a number of Muslims to his kabbalistic views, and in converting many Jews to Islam, thus forming a Judaeo-Turkish sect whose followers implicitly believed in him.

Gradually, the Turks tired of Shabttai's schemes. He was deprived of his salary, and banished from Adrianople to Constantinople.

In a village near the latter city, he was one day discovered singing psalms in a tent with Jews, whereupon the grand vizier ordered his banishment to Dulcigno (today called Ulcinj), a small place in Montenegro, where he died in solitude.

The disaster of the false messiah Shabbtai Zevi caused seventeenth century rabbis to legislate that kabbalah should be studied only by married men over forty, who were also scholars of Torah and Talmud. The medieval rabbis wanted the study of kabbalah limited to people of mature years and character.

CHAPTER NINE

More *dibbukim* accounts

The next account is from the writings of Rabbi Chayim Vital, the student of the holy *Arizal*.

It took place in 1609 and describes a spirit that entered into the daughter of Rafael Anaf of Damascus. Rabbi Vital arrived at the place of the incident on the Sabbath night and describes the events that followed. This is only a summary of what happened.

They asked the spirit: "Who are you?" and he said: "I am Rabbi Piso. Why did you light only two candles? You should have lit many candles for all of the angels and souls of the righteous that came with me to accompany and protect me . . . I am not like the other spirits, for I am both wise and righteous. I came with only one small sin that I still need to repair. I have also came to help you make repentance for the many sins that you committed . . .

I died thirty-five years ago and rose to my place in the Garden of Eden, and I have dwelled there ever since. Yet, there remains one small thing to repair.

I came to correct it, and woe unto anyone who is not careful in this world to avoid even the smallest sin. He shouldn't be like me and go through what I have . . .

And so you residents of Damascus: You do not have the portion in the world to come for several reasons . . . Your women also walk about boldly in immodest clothing and disgraceful jewelry . . . putting on all kinds of perfumes that arouse men's desire, and they do this in the markets and streets to show off their beauty . . . ."

* * *

Here is another true story which happened relatively recently. It is about a young Jewish couple in Europe who had just gotten married. They didn't have much money. All they had was the wife's dowry. The wife's parents had a business, and since the husband was a Torah scholar and studied all day, the father in law provided for them. As years went by, the father in law lost his business and couldn't provide for them anymore.

The wife, though had an idea: "Let's take the dowry that my father gave us and open a store. I will be there everyday, besides two hours a day when you will be in charge. All the rest of the time you can continue studying Torah just as you did until now". And so they agreed on the plan.

The first three months went just as they had intended, but then the husband's two hours became four, and the four hours became eight, until he was at the store the whole time. He didn't even have enough time to open a book.

On Saturday night, after midnight, a fierce blizzard was raging outside. The wife went outside to empty a bucket of dirty water and returned to the house chocking and unable to speak. Her husband ran to get a doctor, but the doctor didn't know what to do. The next day, her husband took her to other doctors, and even to specialists in Vienna, but nothing helped. Rumors spread that it might be a *dibbuk*.

They traveled to the village of Stutchin, in Galicia, to the home of a Kabbalist by the name of Rabbi Mendel, to whom people would travel in order to treat such matters.

When they arrived, Rabbi Mendel asked the *dibbuk* something and heard a voice answer. (Whenever the *dibbuk* would speak, the woman's stomach would swell up, but her lips would not move as the voice emerged). Everyone there was frightened and said: "Ah! Here is the *dibbuk*!".

But the righteous Rabbi Mendel wondered if it really was a *dibbuk*. So he asked it: "Who goes with you? (I.e. are you bound to a particular soul?)

And it said: "Five destroying angels". "What are their names?" he asked it. It told him their names, and Rabbi Mendel agreed that this was indeed a real *dibbuk*.

He began to ask it questions about who it was and where it came from and so on. It answered him that it had lived several decades ago, and that it had been a young man from the town of Brisk. The young man had traveled to Africa, where his friends had a bad influence on him, and he ended up transgressing all the laws of the Torah. Once he was traveling in a carriage and fell out and was killed. His spirit had wandered throughout the world until that very day.

Rabbi Mendel asked him why he had not repented of his deeds in the seconds before he died. He responded that in his fear and surprise during the fall, he had forgotten to repent.

Afterwards, he asked the spirit why it had chosen this woman out of all possible victims upon whom to inflict such suffering. It began to laugh, saying that the mother of the woman and the mother of the husband (both of whom had already died) had pressed heaven to bring suffering upon her so that she would not suffer even more in this world or the world-to-come, because she had caused her husband to stop studying Torah.

When he heard this, Rabbi Mendel asked the husband to promise that he would return to Torah study, and the husband promised. Rabbi Neta, the father of the possessed woman, also promised to study sections of the *Mishnah* in memory of the young man who had become a *dibbuk*—

in addition to dedicating a certain number of candles to be lit in the synagogue in his memory.

Then Rabbi Mendel gathered a quorum of ten men in his room to recite Psalms while he stood in the back of the room and recited certain phrases. He sat the woman in a chair in the middle of the room, and suddenly she rolled out of the chair, fell on the ground, and a loud voice emerged from her saying *Shema Israel*. A fingernail of one of her pinkies split (where the *dibbuk* left her body), and a pane of glass broke in a nearby window. Then all was quiet again.

Rabbi Elyahu Lopian who was present there added that the *dibbuk* at times screamed out in the presence of Rabbi Mendel so loudly, and with such a terrifying sound that everyone who heard him was frightened. He said that the destroying angels were waiting to tear him apart as soon as he left the woman's body (destroying angels do not have permission to touch the soul of an evil person as long as he or she is in a living body).

A few moments later, the *dibbuk* began to speak mockingly, in such raw, ugly language that the people around had to cover their ears in order to avoid hearing such disgusting talk.

They asked it to explain itself, because just moments before it had been crying out for help with a terrified voice. Why was it now speaking to them horribly? It answered: "Listen, if you don't repent and your deeds are not purified of sin, then the spirit continues to pursue evil just as it did below. These were the words of the *dibbuk*.

Rabbi Elyahu concluded by saying: "We can learn from this story the awful power of desire (for evil). Even its great fear of five destroying angels that it saw could not stop the *dibbuk* from speaking the type of vile and disgusting words that it was accustomed to speak while alive.

The young woman and her husband eventually moved to Israel. They lived in Tel Aviv and had children and grandchildren. They took the broken window pane with them as a reminder of what happened and as proof of their story.

* * *

Another incident happened during the life of the Chafetz Chaim, in the year 1909. Every year on Purim, Rabbi Elchanan Wasserman would tell the account just as he had witnessed it himself. Here is the account in his own words:

"On the road from Eisiskes to Vilna—two miles from Eisiskes—there is a village called Streltsi and next to it is a village called Pasvalys, and a Jew named Nachum lived there.

Nachum and his fourteen year old daughter came to Radin to the Chafetz Chaim. His daughter was sick and the father claimed that she had a *dibbuk* inside her. The father described how the spirit had entered his daughter and this is what he said:

After Chanukah, in the month of Tevet (about two months earlier), a horse fell and died in our barn. As soon as we heard this, all of the members of the household went outside in a panic, my daughter included. When she came back from the barn, she was drenched with sweat and drank cold water. From that moment on she was sick.

At first, she had powerful cramps. Then she would collapse senseless to the floor. When this happened to her, she was unaware of what was going on. She only knew that she was weak because of her suffering. Then she would hear a singing voice coming from her, and then she would speak.

"The voice told me that it (the spirit that had entered the girl) had belonged to a twelve year old Jewish girl who had lived with elderly parents. Her actions brought her to the point that she converted. She lived in a small town at the time, and the Jewish children would chase after her calling her a heretic. She fell in with a group of Jew-haters and they killed two Jewish children. Five years later, when she was seventeen, she died, and she was judged by the Supernal Court.

The spirit explained to me that it had wandered in the world ever since. At the beginning of its wandering (immediately after the young woman's death) it had entered inside the image of her gravestone. When the stone broke, it entered into a nearby tree. The tree was cut down, and in the end it entered into a stone that had been in the barn. When the horse stood on the stone, it immediately died. From the horse it entered into a glass of water . . . .

Then the spirit continued: "When all of you ran into the barn, I saw you. I also saw your daughter, but I didn't want to look at her". The spirit also said that Passover that year would mark five years since its "death", and that it would remain in the world for another ten years.

I asked it: "But what do you want from my daughter?" The spirit answered in a sad voice: "Rabbi Nachum, don't you know how terrible things are for me?"

I asked again: "It's terrible for you because you sinned, but what is my daughter guilty of?" It answered: "A girl like that needs to say a blessing when she drinks water. If she had said the blessing, I never could have entered her!".

This is what the father Nachum told Rabbi Elchanan, who now describes the events that took place in Radin the day after the father and daughter arrived there:

"On the eve of Sabbath, I was studying with Rabbi Naftali Tropp and Rabbi Yosef Kuller in the attic where they studied *Kodshim* (a section of the Talmud). As they were learning, the Chafetz Chaim came and asked if we could go see the girl with the *dibbuk* inside of her. We responded to the request of our teacher and all three of us went to the home of Rabbi Yitzchak Tzvi the Beadle. When we arrive, many people had already gathered.

I asked the spirit: "Who are you?" It replied: "A person" I continued: "Where are you from?" It answered: "From the dirt". [The spirit stopped speaking at this point, or Rabbi Elchanan stopped asking questions].

That Sabbath evening, Rabbi Eliyahu Deuschnitzer and Rabbi Yerucham were with the young woman and they spoke with the *dibbuk*.

Rabbi Eliyahu asked it: "Who is appointed over you?"

"Demons" it said.

"What are their names?" he asked.

"Why do you need to know that?" it answered, and then it continued: "When I enter any object or body, I can hide like I am in a place of refuge. Yet they wait for me, and as soon as I emerge, they strike me and chase me out".

Rabbi Eliyahu also told me that when the voice spoke, they looked into the young woman's mouth and saw that her tongue did not move on its own. Another force moved it.

Rabbi Ephraim Aharon Goldberg of Monolishak, who then studied in Radin, testified before me that he himself heard Rabbi Eliyahu ask the spirit: "If the souls of the wicked can rest on the Sabbath in their realm, why don't you rest on the Sabbath?"

It answered that only those who rested on Sabbath in the earthly realm can rest on the Sabbath in the next world. But those spirits that did not rest on Sabbath in this world could not rest on the Sabbath later. Then [Rabbi Elchanan continues] I requested that whenever the spirit began to speak, I should be notified.

On the Sabbath afternoon, they called for me, saying that the *dibbuk* was starting to speak. I quickly walked there. I asked the spirit: "Do you know who the Chafetz Chaim is?"

"I do. He is a great teacher of Torah!"

Then I asked it: "If he asks you to come out of the girl, will you listen to him?"

"I will listen" she responded.

I said: "In truth, he requests that you leave".

"Then I will leave" she replied.

I asked: "When will you come out?"

She said: "Tonight".

I asked: "After you come out of the sick girl, will you return to her?"

This is exactly how the *dibbuk* replied to my question: "If you say *Kaddish* afterwards I won't go back into her. If you don't say *Kaddish*, I will go back into her. And if not into her, then into her sister".

I kept asking her questions:

"Who should say *Kaddish* for you?"

She answered: "Two Rabbis" (which we took to mean two members of the *Kollel*)

"And for how long should they say *Kaddish*?"

"One week" it said. Then she asked me: "From what place in the body should I leave the sick girl?"

I didn't know what to say. People standing there told me to tell her to leave from the girl's pinky, so that is what I told her.

Then another young man came to try to speak to her. She said: "I will not speak to you".

While we were praying the evening prayers at the close of the Sabbath, just after the recitation of the *Shema*, in the middle of the blessing "*Emet V'emunah*" people entered and said that it (the spirit) was just leaving the body of the girl. At the time of its departure, there were three people standing with her and this is what they told:

The sick girl began screaming "It hurts me here!" and then she pointed to her shoulder and yelled, "Here!" and then "My arm hurts!"

Then her hand swelled up, and then just her pinky on the same hand . . . . Afterwards, we heard the sound of glass breaking, and we saw that the window had broken where the *dibbuk* has flown out. All of this happened in the house of Rabbi Pollack, the teacher.

And since that moment, the girl had experienced uncontrollable spasms for several hours. Everyone waited until Sunday evening—about a twenty-four hour period.

When people saw that she was no longer suffering from the disease and that she had returned to normalcy, she and her father returned home.

After all of this, the Chafetz Chaim directed us to form a *minyan* in the attic where they had studied *Kodshim*, and he joined us.

When we finished the prayers, we studied sections of the *Mishnah* on behalf of the spirit.

Rabbi Eliyahu and Rabbi Gershon of Salant said *kaddish* for the spirit for one week, until the time for the reading of the *Purim Megillah*.

CHAPTER TEN

Ghosts

What are ghosts exactly?

There is not much available information about ghosts, and we don't understand the dynamics of ghosts. I am sure you have heard stories about haunted homes and the like. After all, it doesn't make sense. One is either a living human being or dead in the grave. Once the body is in the grave, the soul should be either in Heaven, Hell or the *Sling Shot*.

Ghosts cannot be spirits in *Sling Shot* because these spirits have no peace and are constantly being pursued by malevolent angelic beings and demons. They cannot just show up. So what are these apparitions of ghostly figures, man or woman, appearing?

There is a famous story of President Lincoln's ghost appearing in the White House reported by trustworthy eyewitnesses. In many places in America and the world, ghosts were observed and seen.

For the following 12 months after the soul departs from the body, the *Nefesh* (Hebrew—one part of the soul) is still attached to this physical world. If we had *spiritual eyes* to see, we could see the *Nefesh* on the grave. If the bones of the deceased are still in the grave, his *Nefesh* is still there, and their spiritual presence is there.

The Five Levels and Names of The Soul

From the teachings of Arizal, we learn that our soul is comprised of five levels and five names. Each of these levels represents a different level of light that originated from *Ein Sof*, the infinite light emanating out from God.

From the lowest level up, they are: *Nefesh, Ruach, Neshama*, Chaya and *Yechida*. Translated they are:

Nefesh—(that which has come to) Rest—is the layer that enlivens the body. The soul light comes to rest on the level called *Nefesh*.

Ruach—wind—is the soul light as it leaves the stage of *Neshama*, like a breath blown out of the mouth of a person. The *Ruach* provides emotion. It can be translated as spirit.

Neshama—is derived from the word *Neshima* which means breath—it is the layer that provides intellect. This level of soul is said to be like a breath in the mouth of God, so to speak. In other words, God's breath.

Chaya—life—It is considered to be the life force of all that comes after it. It is the Living Essence.

Yechida—singular—It is Unique Essence or Unity. On the level of *Yechida*, the light is still very sublime and unified. On the level of *Chaya*, it is less so.

The *Chaya* and *Yechida* are the *Makifim*, the surrounding levels of the soul.

In the *Zohar* 3:25a we find that "the *Nefesh* is bound to the *Ruach*, the *Ruach* to the *Neshama*, and the *Neshama* to the Blessed Holy One". The three thus form a sort of chain, linking man to God.

The idea of these three parts is best explained on the basis of the verse: "God formed man out of the dust of the earth, and He blew into his nostrils a breath of life" (Genesis 2:7). This is likened to the process of blowing glass, which begins with the breath (*neshima*) of the glassblower, flows as a wind (*Ruach*) through the glassblowing pipe, and finally comes to rest (*Nefesh*) in the vessel that is being formed. The *Neshama* thus comes from the same root of *Neshima*, meaning breath, and this is the "breath of God".

The *Nefesh* comes from a root meaning "to rest" and therefore refers to the part of the soul that is bound to the body and "rests" there.

Ruach means a wind, and it is the part of the soul that binds the *Neshama* and *Nefesh*.

When a person dies, the *Ruach* and *Neshama* rip themselves away from the *Nefesh* and return to their place above. The *Nefesh*, however, is the only spiritual element that stays in the body after death. It is called *Hevel Ha-atzamot*—the "vapor of the bones"—which remains dormant until the resurrection of the dead, as explained by the *kabbalah*. It maintains its connection with the *Ruach*.

Our ability to stand erect while awake is due to the soul's "support" of the physical body and its resistance against the pull of gravity. When the soul departs at the moment of death, the body loses its ability to withstand the force of gravity and is overcome. This is the reason why a dead body weighs a little more than it did during life. As the *Talmud* says: "A living thing holds itself (up)."

We visit the graves of the deceased because there is a direct connection from that place to the *Ruach* and *Neshama* of the person in Heaven.

*   *   *

Many buildings, streets and other places were built over what used to be cemeteries. Sometimes, people who were buried in these cemeteries come back as ghosts for some reason. They do not have complete rest and haven't arrived yet to their final destination.

Some of them have been killed or murdered and come back as ghosts. Usually, these were people that did not deserve to be killed or murdered.

Many of these ghosts appear because they will have no rest or peace until their murderer is caught.

Some ghosts appear for a certain mission. These ghosts do not appear as ghosts as you know them, but actually appear to us as a living human being, with human flesh.

*   *   *

This next account actually happened to Rabbi Elyiahu Kin's grandfather of blessed memory, who told his uncle about it. He was in Israel. He took a bus and in the bus, he suddenly saw his mother which has passed away ten years earlier. She was wearing the same scarf that she wore when she was still alive.

He looked again as if to make sure that it was her and not someone who looked like her, and sure enough, it was her. He went and sat next to her on the bus and started talking to her. "Hello, how are you?" and he went on and on, but she would not say a word.

Eventually, the bus stopped and she got off the bus. He immediately followed her and tried to talk to her again, and that's when she disappeared. Poof! As if she has never appeared. His grandfather had no explanation for this incident.

Sometimes these ghosts will speak to us and sometimes they won't. There is always a purpose and reason for any apparition.

When deceased people appear in a dream, they have to have permission to disclose information or what they want from us. Only then can they appear in our dreams.

Ghosts are at times figures which appear passing in a room that we can't quite catch. They pass by very quickly and you positively know that you saw something.

It's hard to believe because it doesn't happen very often, and it's hard to explain and "digest" in our physical existence.

The Rabbis explain that God doesn't want us to see everything because we could go crazy.

In order to make it more graspable, we can imagine what the air would look like if we were able to see the infinite number of bacteria on every object floating in the air, as well as endless flow of radio waves, infrared light, and various kinds of radiation that can be collected and translated to images and sound. We would be afraid to move.

So too, the air is filled with the spirits of people who have left their physical bodies, as well as other spiritual creatures described by the *Tanach* (5 books of Moses) and the Sages (and are now beginning to be known to scientists as well).

God has graciously limited our vision so that, for the most part, we cannot see more than what is required. All those other things, which would disturb us and effect our ability to function, remain invisible.

Some people have experienced seeing ghosts occasionally. A major event must have happened there for it to occur.

Many ghostly apparitions occurred in England.

Here are some wild and hair-raising incidents cited in a book by the paranormal researcher Michael Goss, author of *The Evidence for Phantom Hitch-Hikers.*

In October 1979, Roy Fulton from Liverpool, England, was traveling on a deserted stretch of foggy road, "Paradise Lane" near Stanbridge in the area of Bedfordshire, England. He stopped his car to pick up a man with a deathly pale face. Roy asked him where he wanted to go. Goss writes, and the traveler did not say a word, just pointed with his hand in the direction of the nearest town.

After a few minutes, Roy turned to offer the hitchhiker a cigarette. To his shock, he discovered that the passenger's seat was empty. Roy slammed on the brakes and turned the car around to travel in the other direction, afraid that the man has, somehow, fallen out and hurt himself.

When he found absolutely no trace of the hitchhiker, he contacted the police and reported the incident.

The police officers organized a search of the area, but all was in vain. The man had disappeared as if the ground had swallowed him up.

*   *   *

In July 1974, businessman Maurice Goodenough was driving in the area of the Blue Bell Hill in Southern England. To his surprise, he saw the shape of a young woman caught in the glare in his headlights, straight in the path of his rapidly approaching vehicle.

He put on the brakes, but it was too late—his car ran into the girl. He jumped out of the car and found her injured on the road, her legs damaged and her forehead covered with blood, writes Goss. "Mommy" she mumbled once or twice.

Goodenough carried her to the side of the road, covered her with a blanket, and then ran towards his car to try to go for help. But when he returned with the police, the young woman had disappeared. Only the blanket remained.

*   *   *

In another incident in England, the residents of the village of Nanny were hysterical when drivers began reporting sightings of ghosts that had begun to take the form of travelers in the backseats of their cars.

It seemed that all of the incidents had taken place when people were driving along a narrow road where, in the 16th century, a number of criminals had been executed by hanging.

There is a possibility that some of these souls did not have complete rest and were still attached to that road.

The *nefesh,* the portion of the soul that still hovers over the grave, returns and appears at the site of their death.

In 1924, two sailors were killed during an accident on the SS Watertown, an American ship near Panama. In the days that followed, many sailors claimed to see the faces of the dead sailors near the ship. A ship captain took a picture, in which the two dead sailors appeared. The picture was examined by experts in a photo lab that tests for photographic authenticity. The photo was deemed authentic.

* * *

Here is another true story about a Jewish ghost:

About 50 years ago, there was a very learned Torah scholar who devoted his whole life to studying Torah. He was a lonely man. This man never got married and never had children. He was given a room to live in and study, at Rabbi Noach Movshowitz' home, in the city of Malstovka, Poland.

He eventually passed away an old man. One day, one of the children opened the door to the old man's former room and was amazed to see the deceased sitting at his table, studying Talmud in the same place he always had, as if he were alive.

The child became terrified and ran away. Another time, another child opened the door and saw the deceased again, just as described above.

They told this account to Rabbi Noach, who then went into the room. When he saw the deceased, he said to him: I request that you stop coming here, because it scares the children".

He never came again.

Why would he appear in the first place? There must have been a reason. Since he never married and had no children, he had no continuity so to speak. Something was lacking in this man's life and he was not at peace with himself.

There is a possibility that his apparition was to convey a request for his soul's correction. He felt as if he had accomplished nothing and wanted Rabbi Movshowitz to do something for him. Otherwise, what was his connection to the room? He should be resting in peace in the cemetery. Instead of coming as a *dibbuk*, he came back as a ghost.

*   *   *

Another account is told by Rabbi Shabttai Yudelevitz, of Jerusalem.

One of the outstanding students at the Etz Chayim Yeshiva in Volozhin (Poland) became ill and required medical treatment.

He packed his bags in order to travel to his parents' home. One of his friends from the yeshiva accompanied him the entire way.

When evening came, they arrived at a certain town and decided to stay at an inn. In the morning, the owner of the inn gave them their bill. The sick boy counted his money and saw that he was about seven cents short of the total.

The owner of the inn said that he trusted him to come back another time, to pay the small difference. They continued on their way until they arrived to the house of the sick boy's parents. This is where the friend parted from the sick boy with wishes of a speedy recovery.

The sick boy remembered the debt from the inn and gave the amount to his friend, so that on his way back to the yeshiva, he would pay the innkeeper.

The latter promised that he would take care of the debt, and they parted in peace. In the meantime, the boy's illness worsened and after a short time, he died.

When the sad news reached the yeshiva, they wept and eulogized him, for he surely would have been one of the great scholars of their generations.

In the Volozhin yeshiva, the sound of Torah study never stopped. There were rotating shifts of students twenty-four hours a day. This custom was in accordance to the teachings of the Head of the yeshiva, Rabbi Chayim of Volozhin, based on the verse: "If my covenant (i.e. the Torah) is not maintained day and night, then I have not set laws of heaven and earth". That is, if the world were to be devoid of Torah study for even a moment, all of the worlds would be completely destroyed.

Thus, even a single individual can uphold all of the worlds by virtue of his pure-hearted Torah study. How can a person's heart not be set aflame by such a wondrous thing!

One evening, past midnight, Rabbi Chayim was walking through the halls of the yeshiva, observing, assisting and encouraging the students in their studies.

Suddenly, to his great shock, he came eye to eye with the boy who had died, walking towards him.

Rabbi Chayim did not become flustered, but approached the deceased and offered him his hand. "Shalom—Greetings! How is your judgment going in heaven?" Rabbi Chayim asked. The deceased explained to him that when he had arrived at his heavenly trial, they began to weigh all his sins and merits. It soon became apparent that he was free of sin. His judgment was sealed and he immediately entered the Garden of Eden.

Yet, when he came to the gates of Eden, the Accuser stood there, closing the gate in his face and shouting that he should not be allowed to enter, for he had stolen money. To the shock of the angelic entourage, the Accuser revealed that this young man had left the world with a debt of seven cents to that innkeeper.

Even though the boy was not directly responsible, because he had entrusted the debt to someone else, it mattered little to the Accuser. He knew only one thing: the owner of the inn was left seven cents short of his bill. Nor did the owner plan to forget this debt, but believed that it would be paid off at some point.

A debate ensued in the heavenly court, and it was decided that though, on the one hand, the boy was not guilty—because he had done all within his power—the owner was still left in a fix. So in an unusual turn of events, the boy was given permission to appear as a human being before his rabbi, and to request that he take care of the debt. All of these words were told directly to Rabbi Chayim.

Rabbi Chayim promised that he would take care of the matter and the boy suddenly disappeared. Rabbi Chayim called his friend and asked if he had received the money to pay the debt. His friend was upset when he realized he had forgotten to make this small payment. He traveled back to the inn and paid the debt.

The deceased was never seen again, for he had found peace in the upper realms.

* * *

Another account is related concerning the great sage and holy man, Rabbi Yosef Chayim Sonnenfeld, Rabbi of Jerusalem.

This incident took place in Pressburg, Hungary—known today as Bratislava, the capital of Slovakia—during the period when Rabbi Yosef Chayim was teaching at the Ktav Sofer Yeshiva. This is what happened:

Over a period of many years, it had became the custom of a respectable businesswoman to make occasional, large donations to the yeshiva, on the condition that the yeshiva would ensure that kaddish was being said for poor souls that had no one to pray for them. The yeshiva would appoint a young man to be responsible for saying kaddish for all these souls.

At a certain point, the woman's husband died. Because they had managed the business together, his death damaged their prosperity to the point that the business eventually had to close.

The woman's economic situation worsened, until eventually, her two daughters had no funds left for their dowries, and did not know where to go for help.

The woman carried her sorrow in silence and bravely accepted her fate. There was only one thing she could not accept—that the kaddish, which she had subsidized for so many years, would now be cancelled due to the lack of funding.

With great bitterness, she approached the administrators of the yeshiva and requested that the yeshiva continue the tradition of reciting this kaddish, until the time came when God would restore her ability to pay for the service.

The heads of the yeshiva were very moved by her pure-hearted goodness, and agreed to her request. This filled the widow with joy, and a spark of happiness glimmered in her eyes as she left the yeshiva building. From that moment on, her burdens began to lighten, and even the situation of her two daughters began to feel less heavy.

From the moment when the recitation of kaddish was promised to her, she lacked nothing in the world.

Regarding her two daughters, she was sure that God, who protects widows and orphans, would have mercy upon them, finding them matches and seeing to their needs.

She had barely stepped onto the street, when an old Jew with a shining face stood across from her, his beard white and glimmering like snow.

The woman was startled by the otherworldly light radiating from the stranger's face. Her surprise increased seventy-fold when he came towards her and inquired about her condition and the condition of her daughters.

The woman sighed sadly as she revealed to the man her bitter fate— her fall from prosperity and her inability to properly marry off her daughters.

"How much money do you think you need for the expenses of your daughters' weddings?" the old man asked. The woman was astonished at the question and replied: "Why does his honor need to know? What does it matter?" But she hesitantly told him the amount she assumed she would need anyway.

The man pulled out a checkbook and wrote a check for the woman to cash at a local bank. The check was for the exact sum she had mentioned.

Before he signed the check, he made one request. "Because this amount is a substantial one," he said, "it would be best for me to sign it in the presence of two witnesses that will see with their own eyes that it is my personal signature on the check and verify this fact with signatures of their own".

Excited and confused by what was happening, the woman went up the stairs of the yeshiva and asked two young men to come with her.

The old man told them to watch how he signed the check. For extra securities' sake, he requested that they bring him a piece of paper upon which they too could sign, as evidence that everything was done properly. Afterwards, he gave the check to the woman and told her to deposit it in the bank the following morning.

The entire situation seemed strange and inexplicable to the woman. Why was this strange old man, previously unknown to her, suddenly so generous? Why did he show such a big heart, to cover all of the expenses needed to marry off her daughters? Despite her doubts, she was eager to try her luck at the bank the next morning; her heart pounding in her chest as she arrived.

After the bank clerk looked at the check, he gazed up at the woman with utter astonishment.

Uncomfortable and more than a little buffled, he looked at the check again several more times. Fumbling a bit, the clerk then requested that the woman remain at the counter while he went into the office of the manager and owner of the bank.

Then, something very dramatic happened.

When the manager saw the check, he fainted and fell from his chair!

There was chaos in the bank. The other clerks who had heard about the incident quickly took the woman into a side room under watch of a security guard, so that she would not try to escape. Everyone assumed that a case of forgery was at hand.

After the manager of the bank had collected himself, he asked to see the woman who had presented the check to deposit. When she entered, he asked her with astonishment how she had received the check.

"I received it yesterday from a respectable Jew with a kind face" she said., apologizing. "And there are even two witnesses from the yeshiva who can attest to this. They saw him write the check" said the woman.

"Could you identify this man if I showed you a picture of him?" asked the manager. "Of course I could identify him" she said.

"And I have no doubt that the two young men could identify him as well".

The manager asked that he be brought the portrait of his deceased father. When the picture was placed before the woman, she pointed at it without hesitation, indicating that this was the man who had given her the check.

The manager ordered that the check be processed and let the woman go.

After she left, the manager explained to the workers the nature of the strange mystery that had just transpired.

The man who had given the check to the woman was none other than his father who had died ten years earlier. The night before, the father had appeared to the son in a dream and said these words to him:

"Know that ever since you left the path of Judaism, and stopped saying *kaddish* for me, my soul has not known a moment's rest. Not until this anonymous woman came and requested that *kaddish* be said for souls that had no one to pray for them. From the *kaddish* that was said in the yeshiva—by the demand and commitment of that woman—my soul finally found peace and comfort."

The woman will appear tomorrow at your bank with a check that I gave to her to cover the expenses of her marrying off her two daughters".

When I woke up this morning, I was still stunned by the dream. I told it to my wife and she laughed the whole matter off. Then the woman with the check came to prove that the dream really was true after all.

Rabbi Yosef Chayim Sonnenfeld concludes:

"Who were those two young men from the yeshiva?

I was the younger one and my friend, Rabbi Yehudah Greenwald was the other. The bank manager soon returned to a traditional Jewish life, and his wife converted to Judaism, and they merited building a fine Jewish home".

* * *

In a remarkably similar incident, the American psychiatrist and near-death expert, Elizabeth Kubler-Ross, tells how a certain Mrs. Schwartz—whom she tended to before she died—appeared to her *after* the funeral, looking exactly as she had during her life.

Dr. Kubler-Ross was about to quit her job in hospice care when Mrs. Schwartz appeared to her. She wanted to thank Kubler-Ross for all of the good she had done on her behalf, as well as encourage her to continue her important work with the dying.

Kubler-Ross was overwhelmed, certain that she was seeing things. To be sure, she requested that the person addressing her sign her name on a piece of paper. The signature and the handwriting were later verified by family members as belonging to Mrs. Schwartz.

Kubler-Ross stated that this was one of the strangest and most incredible experiences of her life.

*   *   *

A Dead Man Comes to Help Save the Life of a Relative

When the famous kabbalist and holy man, the Baba Sali, died in 1984, a group of Spinka Hassidim were in a terrible traffic accident on their way back from the funeral in Netivot. Four people died in the accident.

The one passenger who survived, despite his nearly fatal injuries, was Avish, the eleven year old son of Grand Rabbi Yaakov Yosef of Spinka.

At the time of the accident, a taxi cab drove by, stopping to help with the rescue efforts that ultimately saved the boy's life.

In the years that followed, the taxi driver remained in contact with the boy's family, and always attended their joyous occasions.

One day, he mentioned something that had troubled him ever since the accident. "As soon as I started to help with the rescue, there suddenly appeared at my side a man with a face with a special glow, who began to recite psalms. I told him that he could help me if he wanted, but if not, he should stand to the side to pray.

During the whole time following the accident, I couldn't stop thinking about how he had come, out of nowhere, and for all these years, I can't stop wondering who he really was".

The driver was certain that he remembered the man's face clearly. One of the family members brought out a photo album with many pictures of people from the family. The driver looked at the pictures without recognizing anyone, yet he insisted that the image of the man was etched in his memory in the clearest way possible.

When they were just about ready to stop looking at the photographs and had all but given up, the driver pointed to one of the pictures and said:

"That's the man I saw at the accident. I am sure of it".

The family members were shocked. The man to whom the driver had pointed was none other than a family member from the previous generation—

The righteous Grand Rabbi of Spinka, author of the book *Chakal Yosef,* who was murdered by the Germans, on May 29, 1942.

This was the man that the driver identified as the person who had come to pray during the efforts to save the young boy's life.

"He came from heaven to pray that the child would live" said the excited driver.

*   *   *

A Little Girl Appears To Save Her Mother's Life

One very cold snowy winter night, a doctor was asleep in bed, after a very long tiring day.

Suddenly, he was being awakened by a little girl that appeared near his bed, asking him and pleading with him to go to her house and help her mom who is gravely ill.

It was very late at night and the doctor was exhausted. But the little girl was so cute and so sincerely concerned that the doctor couldn't refuse.

He also felt terrible for her mother who might be indeed very sick.

So the doctor got up and walked with the little girl to her house. Little did he know, it was quite a long walk. When they arrived to the house, the little girl pointed to it and just left. How strange!

The doctor walked into the house and went to the sick woman's bedroom where she was laying in her bed extremely sick. He right away assessed her condition, took care of her and managed to save her life.

He then turned to the woman and said to her: "You know, you have a wonderful little girl. She walked alone in the snow for so long just to get to me, so I could come see you. She was very concerned about you. You truly have a great daughter".

The woman said to him: "Doctor, my daughter has been dead for several months now. What are you talking about?"

The doctor replied: "What?" and went on to describe what she looked like, The clothes she was wearing and every detail about her. The woman then asked him to open the dresser's drawer which he did. To his astonishment, he saw the exact clothes the little girl wore, in the dresser.

The little girl apparently was dead and somehow came back to help her mother and save her life.

Spirits do come back sometimes, for a purpose. This story reinforces the fact that the soul doesn't cease to exist after death.

*   *   *

CHAPTER ELEVEN

Angels

Why were angels created? What is their role in creation? Why are they necessary?

What is the difference between an angel and a human being?

An angel is spiritual, therefore not limited by the 5 senses, as opposed to human beings who are limited by their 5 senses: sight, smell, hearing, taste and touch. Angels can see the whole world and predict the future. They are closer to God, the source.

On this planet, planet Earth, there are other forms of life. The *Zohar* says that planet Earth is like an onion—there are various layers, various dimensions—We are solely aware of the physical dimension.

There are other creatures, other creations that are less physical than us, humans. They live with us either on this plane or underground, or above in space. We can't see them. Some of them are called angels and some are called demons.

The bible says: "God vivified every part of the firmament with a particular spirit; immediately all the celestial hosts were formed and found themselves before Him".

This is the meaning of what is said: "With the breath of His mouth He created all their hosts . . . . (Psalms, 33:6)

Several kinds of *Mal'achim* (angels) are mentioned in our prayer book. Some of them are called *Serafim, Ofanim, Chayot HaKodesh.*

The word *Mal'ach* (angel) means *Mesharet*—servant, or messenger.

Angels are God's messengers. They partake in many of the functions of the universe.

God created the world, supervises it and has servants appointed to fulfill certain tasks.

There are the angel of purity (*Tahariel*), the angel of mercy (*Rahmiel*), the angel of justice (*Tzadkiel*), the angel of deliverance (*Padael*) and the famous *Raziel*, the angel of secrets who watches over the mysteries of the kabbalistic wisdom.

The angelic hierarchy begins only in the third world, the world of formation (*Olam Yetzirah*), the place occupied by the planets and celestial bodies.

The chief of all angels is the angel *Metatron*, so called because his place is immediately below the throne of God, and who alone constitutes the world of Creation, or the world of pure spirits (*Olam Habryiah*).

His task is to maintain unity, harmony, and the movement of the spheres.

This is exactly the task of the infinite force which, at times has been substituted for God under the name of "Nature".

The myriads of subordinates under *Metatron's* command have been divided into ten categories.

These angels are to the different divisions of nature, to every sphere and to every element in particular, what their chief is to the entire universe. Thus, one presides over the movements of the earth, another over the movements of the moon, and so on over all other celestial bodies.

One is called the angel of fire (*Nuriel*), another is called the angel of light (*Uriel*), a third presides over the distribution of the seasons, a fourth over vegetation.

In short, all the forces and all the phenomena of nature are represented in the same manner.

In what do human tasks differ from angels' tasks?

The world we live in is called *Olam Ha'Assyiah*—the world of actions—It is very specific and customized.

It is the most physical world we know, and the lowest level in the creation of worlds. A world of deeds and action, where human beings need to perform. In order for deeds to be performed, the world has to be physical.

In the spiritual realm, we do not have the same kind of performance that we have here in the physical realm.

The further we get away from planet earth, the more it becomes less physical and more spiritual.

Human beings have free will because they are partners so to speak in this world of deeds, actions.

God wanted to have humans to do certain deeds to bring them the kingdom of God. If humans do what God instructed them to do, God rewards them for it.

Since humans are being rewarded by being God's partners in creation, God gave humans free will to allow them to either oblige or refuse, to choose between good or evil.

Humans have inclinations—the good and bad inclination—They can rebel, they can refuse. They can choose between good or evil. We have the choice to either be constructive or destructive.

Angels do not have free will. They cannot be destructive. Therefore, they do not have an evil inclination. They are basically programmed so to speak.

Animals as well have no free will. They function with their instincts. Because they were created and born with these instincts, they know for example to run away from fire or any other dangerous situation.

Everything that God created has a purpose. King David came to this realization when he asked God why were spiders created. He couldn't comprehend the purpose of creating spiders.

When King David ran away from Saul, he hid in a cave.

God made a miracle and commanded a spider to cover the cave's entrance with a huge spider web in a matter of minutes, which normally would take months to accomplish.

When Saul came after King David with his army, they saw a huge web covering the cave's entrance and they were all convinced that no one could have entered the cave since the web was intact and untouched. That consequently saved King David's life.

That is when King David realized that there was a need for spiders and that everything that God created has a purpose.

God created angels, therefore there is a need for angels. The same way God wanted to have physical beings in our physical world, He also wanted to have spiritual entities in the spiritual world. What is the spiritual entity's task in the spiritual world? What do they accomplish that is so important?

God has various branches of operation in this world: The legislative branch, the executive branch and the judicial branch.

God is the legislator.

The executive branch involves human beings.

The judiciary branch or operation branch consist of angels and demons. Albeit they dwell in the spiritual realm, their influence is felt in the physical world.

Some angels do not descend to earth. They remain in Heaven. They have a specific function. Other angels are more involved in this world.

Some angels are called *Sarim*—Ministers—Ministers of nations who are in charge of a particular nation.

Every nation has its personal angelic minister. Just like constellations influence someone's life, so do angels influence the nation's fate. They perform what needs to be done.

Some protective angels accompany us. Elijah the prophet for instance is an angel that interacts with people. He actually has been seen.

How can he be seen if he is spiritual? All spiritual entities such as angels and spirits have the ability to materialize when they come down to this world for a purpose or a mission.

The *Kabbala* says that they put on a "suit" so to speak, to enable us to see them. Some angels are destructive and some are protective.

The protecting angels protect and defend us in Heaven when we die.

The destructive angels are called *Malaachei Chabala,* Angels of destruction.

As the verse in Psalms states: *Ose Malaachav Ruchot Umeshartav Esh Lohet*—God has made angels his powerful winds and his servants burning fires—

Sometimes God allows things to happen but He is aware and involved in everything. Even nature which is somewhat basically independent follows rules that God has put into place.

At times, nature will break the rules, and that's when a miracle occurs, a supernatural occurrence which indicates that God is involved in this world.

Let's look at earthquakes for example. The verse says: *Hamabit laaretz vatiraad*—When God looks down at earth, the earth shakes.

The *Gemara* explains why there are earthquakes, tornados, severe thunderstorms etc. These phenomenon are actually destructive angels carrying out God's decrees. It is their mission.

Hakol mesayim Lamelech—Afilu Ruach, Afilu Mezikim—All assist the King, even ghosts and spirits, even harming forces, such as destructive angels and demons.

We can't see angels because we are physical beings and are not capable of seeing spiritual entities. It is one of mankind's limitations.

However, animals and pets can sometimes see spiritual entities that humans cannot see, due to the fact that their senses and perception are more developed and in tune.

Many pets and animals for example will sense that an earthquake is about to occur, something humans cannot do.

It is important to have the right perspective in life. Is there human or Divine intervention? Is there such a thing as a coincidence?

In Judaism, there are no coincidences. Everything happens with divine providence and intervention.

Not only did God create the world, but He is around and supervises the world. We can't always see it because God's miracles are disguised by nature.

CHAPTER TWELVE

Demons

What is a demon?

Demons are half angels and half human. Certain of their functions are angelic and certain are human.

In what way do they resemble angels? They have wings, they can fly and can foretell future events.

They have the ability to transform themselves.

In what way do they resemble humans? They eat and drink, they reproduce and they die.

What do we need them for? Why were they created? There is something very unique about them.

The sages tell us that they were created at the very last stage of creation—On Friday at twilight—right after sundown and right before the Sabbath.

They are incomplete. They have no physical body, that's why they are half angels and half humans.

They were created for a purpose and they have missions.

The *Zohar*, one of the most important books on the *Kabbalah* ever written, distinguished between three types of demons.

Those who are similar to angels, those resembling humans, and those who pay no respect to God, and are like animals.

Demons are said to resemble angels in that they fly and have no permanent physical form. They are said to resemble humans in that they eat, drink, reproduce, and eventually die.

At the end of the sixth day of creation, God created demons, creatures which were to be angel-like. He had made their souls and given them their intelligence and power, but ran out of time before the Sabbath, and so the demons had no bodies, nor were they ever completed.

These demons were His creation, God-fearing, and subject to Him.

However, because of their unfinished state, they became resentful and jealous of humankind. These demons are sometimes referred to as "sublunar", that is earthly demons.

As a general rule, these demons didn't actively seek to harm human beings unless they had a good reason.

For example, if they had been bound against their will or trapped, their home had been trespassed, or they had been provoked. "Demons will torment only people who annoy them" Rabbi Judah he-Hassid wrote in *Sefer Hassidim* (The Book of the Pious).

In another example, Rabbi Judah writes that one must not step on crumbs, for "The demon of poverty resents it when a person steps on breadcrumbs. He says "After this fellow filled his belly with bread, he steps on the leftovers. He would destroy the whole world if he could".

He cites a number of activities that annoy demons, including witchcraft, an activity widely believed to involve the summoning and binding of demons.

It says that G-d inflicts pain, diseases and plagues upon people through these demons. Imperfect beings that inflict pain and suffering for imperfect actions. Their mission is to punish.

Most of them have no hair. It's not easy to see them. They are not around us too much thank God.

If you happen to walk alone where they are, they may harm you. If two people walk together, they won't harm them. If three individuals walk together, they won't appear. They normally don't frequent cities but rural areas.

According to the *Kabbalah*, There is a destructive force that can always accompany a person and that is: a destructive force created by a sin. Certain sins produce certain negative destructive forces just like certain good deeds produce certain protective angels.

Some people have seen demons in dreams. Usually, these dreams are scary and are false dreams. God has many messengers who carry out his orders.

Ashmedai (also known as *Asmodeus*) is often called the Minister of the Jewish demons, and is said to ascend to Heaven to study the Torah. He also seems to have a sense of humor with a mean streak.

There are number of stories concerning him getting the better of King Salomon when the king became brashly self confident with him. One of them goes as follows:

King Salomon had a grand and very beautiful garden in his palace's yard.

In this garden, he had all kinds of animals, beautiful birds, fish ponds with various kinds of fish. King Salomon would walk every morning in his garden and praise God for the magnificent creation He had created.

On one of his habitual morning walks in the garden, King Salomon was unusually lightly dressed, with fewer layers of his royal garments he would normally wear. It was a very hot day. He strolled with pleasure admiring all of God's beautiful creations, and praised Him, as he would every morning.

King Salomon had a tent in his garden where he bound *Ashmedai* with iron chains, so he couldn't harm anyone, due to his extreme power.

Walking along, he happened to pass near *Ashmedai's* tent. The minister of demons saw King Salomon and begged him to release him from the iron chains he was bound to, and to set him free.

King Salomon replied: "First, tell me what is the reason that you are so powerful that God Himself praises the angels and the demons, as the verse says: *Keto'afot Re'em Lo—To'afot* meaning angels, *Re'em* meaning demons.

Ashmedai replied: "How can I show you when my strength is taken away by these chains I am bound to, on which God's name is engraved, and you, Your Majesty, are standing in front of me, and on your finger a gold ring with God's name engraved on it? All of this weakens my power!"

King Salomon heard *Ashmedai's* words, and in his eagerness to know the secret of his power, released him from his chains, and then removed his ring from his finger.

Right away, *Ashmedai* jumped on King Salomon, swallowed his ring and then threw it into the ocean. He then grabbed the king's royal garment, removed King Salomon's crown, spread his wings and flew away. He raised one wing toward the skies, and lowered the other into the abyss, and threw King Salomon a distance of 400 miles away.

King Salomon later on found himself in a middle of a road far away from his palace, and fainted out of fear.

Afterward, *Ashmedai* transformed himself into King Salomon. He wore his royal garments, put his crown on his head, changed his appearance to look exactly like King Salomon, and changed his voice to the king's voice.

He preceded to go to King Salomon's palace and sat on his throne.

The palace's ministers and servants thought he truly was King Salomon.

When the servants would walk in the palace's garden, they wouldn't dare approaching *Ashmedai's* tent out of fear. Therefore, they had no way of knowing what had happened.

When King Salomon awoke from fainting, he recalled everything that happened to him.

He realized that a short time ago, he was surrounded by ministers and important people, and now, he is all dirty and muddy, on the street, like a poor beggar that nobody knows.

He still kept his spirit up and said to God: *"Tzidkatecha Kehararei El, Mishpatecha Tehom Rabbah"*—You lifted me up to the highest mountains, and You threw me way down to the abyss to become a beggar and to sit amongst all the beggars—

You gave me everything, and You took everything away from me. May Your Name be blessed forever and ever!

A few days went by and King Salomon was starving for food and thirsty for water.

The hunger and thirst weakened him, and he had no choice but to join the other beggars he has met, and ask for charity and food from whomever was kind enough to give it.

He walked from town to town, village to village, and called out with a loud voice : "I am King Salomon! I am *Kohelet* (another name for King Salomon) son of David! I was a King over Israel in Jerusalem!"

Everyone that heard him was convinced that he was a mad man, and out of piety for him, would give him food and charity money.

One day, King Salomon knocked on someone's door to beg for food. A woman opened the door for him, and he told her that he was King Salomon. She asked him to come in and served him a plate full of cooked barley.

When he finished his meal, she rushed him out of the house with a stick and hit him on his shoulder, telling him:

"Get out of my house! You are out of your mind! King Salomon is sitting on his throne in Jerusalem. How dare you say that you are King Salomon?"

King Salomon then said: *"Ma Yitron La'Adam Bechol Amalo, Sheya'amol Tachat Hashemesh?*—what is the advantage of human's toiling, that he should toil under the sun.

With tears rolling down his eyes, he went on saying: *"Ze Chelki Mikol Amali"*—this is my lot from all my toiling.

Another time, someone found him in the street and took him to his home. As soon as this person's wife saw him, after he claimed again that he was King Salomon, she wanted him out of the house because she was offended by what King Salomon once said about women: *"Achat Mi'elef Lo Matzati"*—one out of a thousand I couldn't find.

King Salomon listened to what she had to say and then said to her: "I will explain to you what I meant by saying that about women. My intention was good.

If one day an argument or fight shall arise between a couple, the husband cannot claim—I will divorce her and take another wife. And so, they will always live in peace and harmony".

And so, for many months, King Salomon would walk in the land of Israel begging for food and charity, and no one would believe his claims of being the King.

However, there were two people, one a wealthy man, and the other, a poor man, that wondered if he was indeed King Salomon, and didn't treat him like the rest.

One day, the wealthy man approached King Salomon and said to him: "Come to my house to have a copious meal, but make sure the neighborhood kids do not follow you and throw stones at you, so the stones won't be thrown at my windows by accident".

And so, King Salomon did as the wealthy man requested, and made sure that no one will notice him, on his way to the man's house.

The wealthy man's wife prepared a royal meal, with plenty of meat to eat and wine to drink, and all the food imaginable worthy for a king to enjoy.

While he was eating, he would reminisce about the past days of his kingdom, his magnificent royal table in his palace, his many servants and all he once had. He got so sad thinking about it that he burst in tears and left the wealthy man's house.

The next day, the poor man approached him and invited him to join his family for a meal at his house. King Salomon asked him: "Do you wish to invite me or to subject me to what your wealthy friend subjected me to?"

The poor man answered: "I am poor and don't have much to offer you except for some vegetables I have left in my house. Whatever I have to eat, I'll share with you".

King Salomon accepted his offer and went with him.

When King Salomon arrived to the poor man's house, the latter gave him water to wash his hands and feet, and shared with him the little he had of his vegetables.

The poor man then pursued by consoling him and telling him not to feel sad that he became a pauper after being a king, because it's only a temporary situation and that the time will come when he will sit on his throne again. He went on saying that God swore to King David his father that his kingdom will not depart from his seed.

King Salomon was extremely comforted to hear these words of consolation from the poor man. When he finished his meal and got ready to leave the poor man's house, the latter asked him to stay a while longer because he wanted to call his two children so they can perform a dance for him, to bring some joy to him.

The poor man asked his two boys to come out, gave them some sweets, started to sing, and then the children started to dance.

King Salomon couldn't hold his joy and applauded the children.

As the night fell, the poor man invited King Salomon to stay at his house for the night and he accepted. He offered King Salomon his bare straw mattress that had no sheets or pillow, and he himself slept on the floor with his children.

The following day, King Salomon thanked the poor man and parted from him with joy in his heart.

These two incidents were engraved in King Salomon's mind. Later on, when he eventually returned to his kingdom, he stated with great wisdom: "*Tov Aruchat Yerek Ve Ahavah Sham, Mishor Avouss Vessina'ah Bo*"—I would rather have a meal of vegetable surrounded by love—(the poor man's meal), than have a meal of beef surrounded by hatred—(the wealthy man's meal which reminded him of his sorrow).

*　*　*

And King Salomon went on walking from city to city, village to village, to beg for food and charity for months.

He finally reached Jerusalem, and decided to show up before the *Sanhedrin*. So he did, and with great emotion and excitement told them: "I am King Salomon!"

The *Sanhedrin* were astonished from his words and were convinced he was some kind of a mad man, felt sorry for him and chased him out.

But King Salomon didn't give up and persevered. He would show up before them day after day and would try to convince them that he was indeed whom he said he was.

The *Sanhedrin* finally asked him: "If you are indeed King Salomon like you claim you are, who then is sitting on your throne?"

King Salomon replied: "It is *Ashmedai*, the minister of demons!" and told his astonished listeners all that had happened to him.

The wise men of the *Sanhedrin* listened carefully and attentively to his words, and realized that the man talking to them is very wise and not the fool they thought he was. They decided to investigate the matter.

The *Sanhedrin* called in Benayahu Ben Yehoyadaa, the army minister, and asked him if he recently had the chance to be called by the king. Benayahu replied that it has been a very long time since he has been called to see the king. He added that it was strange since he used to be called by the king very often.

The wise men of the *Sanhedrin* went on to investigate and asked the king's ministers, if they had the opportunity to see the king's feet and toes, so they could determine if he had human's feet or demon's feet which resemble chickens' feet. They replied that it has been a long time since they saw his feet because he always wears socks.

The *Sanhedrin* members understood that something wasn't right, and called in King Salomon who was begging for food in the streets to come and see them.

They asked him: "If indeed what you say is true, that you are King Salomon, and that *Ashmedai* expelled you and sits on your throne—then you are King Salomon, the wisest man on earth—Could you give us any suggestion of how to fight him and expel him, because we are afraid of him. With his power, he is capable of destroying the whole city of Jerusalem"

King Salomon replied: "I alone will fight him and expel him from my throne and will cast him to the "darkness" mountains which is his dwelling place. However, to do this, I will need an iron chain on which God's Holy name is engraved, and a gold ring on which God's Holy name is engraved as well".

The *Sanhedrin* agreed to provide him with what he asked for.

King Salomon took the iron chain and the gold ring in his hands and went to the palace. A few strong men accompanied him and among them, the army minister, Benayahu Ben Yehoyadaa. The *Sanhedrin* members joined them as well, to witness what will happen in the king's palace.

When they arrived to the palace, they went in and walked until they reached the king's chambers. And here, walking very slowly and silently, King Salomon opened the door very carefully. *Ashmedai* right away noticed King Salomon, and when he saw the iron chain and the gold ring both with God's Holy name engraved, he disappeared with a big noise and they couldn't see him anymore.

That's when everyone realized that the poor man begging for food and charity in the streets of Jerusalem was indeed King Salomon, and the "man" sitting on his throne was *Ashmedai*, the minister of demons that expelled him from his throne.

From that day on, King Salomon was not as happy and serene as he was prior to his ordeal. He would have nightmares in his sleep, and have tremendous fears reliving in his mind all that he went through. He posted army people and strong men with swords that would guard his chambers at night.

Lilith and Her Offspring

According to legend, before Eve, God made Lilith, much as He made Adam.

Although Adam considered himself the superior, Lilith didn't agree, claiming she was her own person. They quarreled constantly, until finally Lilith became enraged and fled the Garden of Eden.

She settled in a cave, where her relations with demons produced the first of her children. Unlike the "original" demons, Lilith and her hybrid children are typically malicious and actively seek to harm humans in one way or another.

The Sitra Akhra

Sitra Akhra could be translated "the other side".

Some philosophers believed that all things were created by and subject to God, including demons.

Others wondered if the things which were so unspeakably evil had their origins in another realm outside of God's command, or at least if there was a place forsaken by God, or where the inhabitants had no respect for God at all.

This produced the idea of *Sitra Akhra*, the closest to a classical Hell, where the inhabitants are purely evil and have completely forsaken God, existing only to satisfy their perverted whims.

The demon *Samael* is sometimes said to live there. Any being from *Sitra Akhra* would be completely evil, malevolent, and very dangerous.

The demons according to the kabbalists, are the grossest and most imperfect forms, the "shell" (*Klipah*) of existence; in short, everything that denotes absenses of life, of intelligence and of order. Like the angels, they form ten degrees where darkness and impurity thicken more and more.

The first two degrees are nothing else but the state in which Genesis represents to us the earth before the work of the six days, meaning absense of all visible form and all of organization.

The third degree is the seat of darkness, the same darkness which in the beginning covered the face of the abyss.

Then follow what are called the seven tabernacles (*Sheva Hechalot*), or so-called hell, which shows us in a systematic outline all the disorders of the moral world and all the torments consequent to them.

There we see every passion of the human heart, every vice and every weakness personified in a demon who becomes the tormentor of those who have been led astray by these faults.

Here—lust and seduction, there—anger and violence, further on gross impurity, the demon of solitary debauches, elsewhere—crime, envy, idolatry and pride.

The seven infernal tabernacles are divided and subdivided infinitely.

For every kind of perversity there is something like a special kingdom and thus the abyss unfolds itself gradually in all its depth and immensity.

The supreme chief of that world of darkness who bears the Scriptural name of "Satan" is called in the Kabbala "*Samael*" (*Sam*—Hebrew—poison), meaning the angel of poison or of death.

The Zohar states positively that the angel of death, evil, desire, satan and the serpent which seduced Eve in the Garden of Eden, are one and the same thing.

Samael is also given a wife who is the personification of vice and sensuality, for she calls herself the chief prostitute or the mistress of debauches (*Eshet Zenunim*).

Ordinarily, they are united into one single symbol called simply the beast.

To reduce this demonology and angelology to the simplest and most general form, the kabbalists recognized in each object of nature, and consequently in all nature, two very distinct elements: one, an inner incorruptible which reveals itself to the intelligence exclusively, and which is the spirit, the life or the form. The other, a purely external and material element that has been made the symbol of forfeiture, of curse and death.

Glossary

Arizal—Acronym for Rabbi Isaac Luria (1534-July 25, 1572) was a Jewish mystic in Safed, Israel. His name today is attached to all of the mystic thought in the town of Safed in 16th century Ottoman Palestine. While his direct literary contribution to the kabbalistic school was minute (he only wrote a few poems), his fame led to the school and all its works being named after him. The main popularizer of his ideas was Rabbi Hayim Vital, who claimed to be the official interpreter of the Lurianic system, though this was disputed by some.

Chafetz Chayim—(Hebrew—Desirer of life). Rabbi Israel HaCohen Kagan (Feb. 6, 1838-1933) was called the Chafetz Chayim, which is the title of his famous work, a book about guarding one's tongue from evil and one's lips from speaking deceit.

Etrog—(Hebrew) the fruit of a citron tree.

Gehenom—(Hebrew)—or *Gehenna*—words used in Jewish and Christian writings for the place where evil people go in the afterlife—Hell.

Gemara—(Aramaic—completion from *gemar*, to complete)—2nd-5th Century CE elaborations. The second part of the *Talmud* consisting primarily of commentary of the *Mishnah*.

Hoshannah Rabbah—(Aramaic—supplication) the seventh day of the Jewish holiday of *Sukkot*, 21st day of *Tishrei*—this day is marked by a special synagogue service, in which seven circuits are made by the worshippers with their *lulav* and *etrog*, while the congregation recites *hoshannot* (supplications).

Kabbalah—(Hebrew—literally, receiving)—Jewish esoteric thought. A discipline and school of thought concerned with the mystical aspect of Judaism. It is a set of esoteric teachings that is meant to explain the relationship between an infinite eternal and essentially unknowable Creator with the finite and mortal universe of His creation.

Kaddish—(Aramaic: holy) refers to an important and central prayer in the Jewish prayer service. The central theme of the *kaddish* is the magnification and sanctification of God's name. In the liturgy, several variations of the *kaddish* are used functionally as separators between various sections of the service.

The term "*kaddish*" is often used to refer specifically to "the mourners *kaddish*", said as part of the mourning rituals in Judaism in all prayer services, as well as at funerals and memorials. When mention is made of "saying *kaddish*", this unambiguously denotes the rituals of mourning.

Kapparot—(Hebrew—atonements) is a traditional Jewish animal sacrifice that takes place on the eve of *Yom Kippur*. Classically, it is performed by grasping a live chicken by the shoulder blades and moving it around one's head three times, symbolically transferring one's sins to the chicken. The chicken is then slaughtered and donated to the poor, preferably eaten at the Pre-*Yom Kippur* feast.

Kolel—(Hebrew) a place where adults gather to engage in serious and joyful Jewish text study, which bonds people together, builds community and fosters spiritual growth.

Lulav—(Hebrew) a ripe, green, closed frond from a date palm tree. One of the three types of branches held together with one type of fruit (*etrog*), and waived in a special ceremony during the Jewish holiday of *Sukkot*.

Midrash—(Hebrew) to investigate or study, is a homiletic method of biblical exegesis (interpretation). The term also refers to the whole compilation of homiletic teachings of the Bible.

Midrash is a way of interpreting biblical stories that goes beyond simple distillation of religious, legal or moral teachings. It fills in many gaps left in the biblical narrative regarding events and personalities that are only hinted at.

Minyan—(Hebrew—to count, number) in Judaism, refers to the quorum of ten required for certain religious obligations.

Mishnah—The first part of the Talmud, containing traditional oral interpretations of scriptural ordinances (*Halachot*), finally codified by Rabbi Akiva, his pupil Rabbi Meir, and his pupil Rabbi Yehuda HaNassi, 1st-2nd Century CE, compiled by the rabbis.

Rashi—The acronym for **R**abbi **Sh**lomo **Y**itzhaki (February 22, 1040-July 13, 1105). *Rashi* was a medieval French Rabbi famed as the author of the first comprehensive commentary on the Talmud, as well as a comprehensive commentary on the *Tanach* (Hebrew Bible). He is considered the "father" of all commentaries that followed on the Talmud and the *Tanach*.

Rosh Hashanah—(Hebrew), literally "head of the year", is a Jewish Holiday commonly referred to as the "Jewish New Year". *Rosh Hashanah* is the first of the High Holidays or *Yamim Noraim* (days of awe) or *asseret yemei teshuvah* (the ten days of repentance) which are days specifically set aside to focus on repentance that conclude with the holiday of *Yom Kippur*

Sanhedrin—(Hebrew) Greek—*synedrion* "sitting together" hence "assembly" or "council"—was an assembly of twenty-three judges appointed in every city in the land of Israel.

The Great *Sanhedrin* was the Supreme Court of ancient Israel. In total, there were seventy-one members. The Great *Sanhedrin* was made up of a Chief/Prince/Leader called *Nasi*, a Vice Chief Justice (*Av Beit*

Din), and sixty nine general members. In the Second Temple period, the Great *Sanhedrin* met in the Hall of Hewn Stones in the Temple in Jerusalem. The Court convened every day except festivals and Sabbath.

Shabttai Zevi—Other spellings include Sabbatai Zevi, Sabetay Sevi (August 1, 1626-possibly September 17, 1676) was a rabbi and kabbalist who claimed to be the long-awaited Jewish Messiah, and later converted to Islam.

Shofar—(Hebrew) a horn used for Jewish religious purposes. *Shofar* blowing is incorporated in synagogue services on *Rosh Hashanah* and *Yom Kippur.*

Sukkah—(Hebrew) is a temporary dwelling that Jews use during the holiday of *Sukkot* (plural for *sukkah*).

Talmud—The collection of writings constituting the Jewish civil and religious law. The *Talmud* consists of two parts—The *Mishnah*, or text, and the *Gemara*, or commentary.

Tefillin—(Hebrew), also called phylacteries, are a pair of black leather boxes containing scrolls of parchment inscribed with verses from the bible. The hand *tefillin*, or *shel yad*, is worn by Jews wrapped around the arm, hand and fingers while the head *tefillin*, or *shel rosh*, is placed above the forehead. They serve as a "sign" and "remembrance" that God brought the children of Israel out of Egypt and serve several purposes in the fulfillment of the scriptural commandments prescribing them to be worn by Jews.

Tikkun—(Hebrew)—correction of the soul.

Tikkunim—(Hebrew) plural for *tikkun.*

Tzitzit—(Hebrew) fringes or tassels worn by observant Jews on the corner of four cornered garments, including the *tallit* (prayer shawl) and *tallit katan*. Since they are considered by Orthodox tradition to be a time-bound commandment, they are worn only by men.

Yeshiva—(Hebrew—"sitting") an institution unique to classical Judaism for Torah study, the study of *Talmud*, rabbinic literature and responsa.

Yom Kippur—(Hebrew), also known in English as the "day of atonement", is the most solemn and important of the Jewish Holidays. Its central themes are atonement and repentance.

Jews traditionally observe this holy day with a 25-hour period of fasting and intense prayer, often spending most of the day in synagogue services

Zohar—(Hebrew—splendor or radiance) the 2nd Century C.E. esoteric interpretation of the Torah by Rabbi Shimon Bar Yochai and his disciples. The Zohar is widely considered the most important work of Kabbalah, or Jewish mysticism. It contains a mystical discussion of the nature of God, the origin and structure of the universe, the nature of souls, sin, redemption, good and evil, and the relationship between God and man.